Fall of Freedom

D. Michael Phillips

InfoNovels
USA

To Lara
America First
With Regards
Mike Phillips

Cover design by Mary Fisher Design
        Illustrations by J.W. Turner

Phillips, D. Michael.
        Fall of Freedom / by D. Michael Phillips.
                p.   cm.

        ISBN 0-9656929-1-4

        Library of Congress Catalog Card Number: 98-75192

InfoNovels
USA

"As our case is new, so we must think anew and act anew. We must disenthrall ourselves, and then we will save our country."

Abraham Lincoln

"Posterity is likely, in my opinion, to see liberalism and all its legislative and social consequences as the working out of a collective death wish."

Malcolm Muggeridge

ACKNOWLEDGEMENTS

Thanks to my friend, Terry Loucks, and his wife Ursula, who encouraged me to write my first novel.

Thanks to another old friend, Charles Bennett, of the Museum of New Mexico, who helped me write accurately about many details concerning the history of Santa Fe and its people.

Thanks to my cousin, Pat Clark, the baby who came to live with us in 1944 following the death of his father, and who grew up to have a fine career as a federal law enforcement officer. He answered many of my questions about weapons and tactics.

Thanks to my uncle, John Davis, who survived a tour of duty in the Pacific as a radioman aboard a B-29 near the end of World War II. As a lifelong New Mexican, he helped make sure that my translations of the Spanish words in the book are correct.

Thanks finally to yet another old friend, Donald S. Noble, Lieutenant Commander U.S. Navy, (retired), a veteran of the war in Vietnam, whose assistance and encouragement were invaluable to me in the completion of this book and who is already helping me to lay the keel of the next one.

DEDICATION

To my wife, Judith, who is the love of my life. She really deserves to be listed as the co-author of this book because she helped and advised me every step of the way. If you find the plot of this book interesting and exciting, you probably have her to thank for it.

NOTE TO THE READER

This is a work of fiction. All of the events, characters and institutions depicted in this novel are entirely fictitious or are used fictitiously.

PREFACE

At the height of World War II when I was only three years old, two young sailors came to our house in Tulsa, Oklahoma, to share my family's carefully rationed Thanksgiving dinner. My mother had arranged for their visit by calling the USO and putting our name on the list of people who were willing to open their homes to lonely servicemen for the holiday.

The two sailors assigned to us were in route to join their ship (unnamed, of course) somewhere on the West Coast. They were very nice young men, friends before they joined the Navy, I think, and slightly exotic to me because they were from some far away place like Pittsburgh. They were quite handsome in their dark blue uniforms with that odd rectangle of buttons on the front of their trousers, and they wore those perky white sailor hats you could fold into all sorts of shapes.

They were charming and well mannered, as I remember, and even helped clean up after the meal. They made a big fuss over me, letting me play with their hats as much as I wanted, and I was quite taken with them both. For weeks after that those dashing young sailors loomed very large in my thoughts. Then, late the following spring, we learned the awful news that both of those fine young men, so cheerful and full of the juice of life, had been killed when their ship was sunk during the Battle of the Coral Sea.

A year and a half after that my uncle, Lt. Thomas P. Clark, from Santa Fe, New Mexico, was flying a low level bombing mission near Hansa Bay in New Guinea. His B-25 was hit by enemy ground fire. Rather than ditch their wounded bomber in the ocean, the crew elected to crash it into a Japanese freighter. Both plane and ship were destroyed in the resulting explosion. My uncle received the Silver Star, awarded posthumously, and my Aunt Diantha, his widow, came to live with us, bringing along her infant son, who would grow up without ever seeing his father or hearing his voice.

That was a long time ago. I have forgotten the names of those two young sailors, and I do not even have a photograph of my courageous uncle, but this book is for the three of them. This book is for them and for all the brave young men who died fighting to preserve our nation and our way of life so many years ago.

D. Michael Phillips
Winston-Salem, North Carolina
1998

THURSDAY
SEPTEMBER NINTH

1

The Lieutenant settled his heavy rifle into a comfortable shooting position and scanned the bustling prairie dog town on the far side of old I-25. Through his telescopic sight he could see dozens of the little rodents standing watch atop the large earthen mounds that marked the entrances to their burrows, or simply sunning themselves in the feeble warmth of the September twilight.

He centered the crosshairs on a particularly fat little male and tried once again to block the pain that radiated from his swollen foot.

"Let's have us a little dry fire drill," he said to his spotter, who had been keeping his own lookout for Fidelista patrols.

The spotter brought his binoculars to bear on the area where his partner was aiming.

"Lots of happy little targets out there," he said

Snipers had been teamed with spotters in this way ever since the army psychologists determined that a man with a companion was far more likely to actually pull the trigger and commit the kind of long distance murder that was required of him if he had someone along side of him to share the guilt.

The two men who composed this particular team were new to the business of killing. Lieutenant Sanford McDowell was a rangy young rifleman from Tennessee, given to long silences and deep thoughts about his duty to God and country, while Corporal Roberto Chavez, was a cheerful young man, shorter than his partner by a head, but possessed of more strength and stamina since he had grown up in the thin air of these mountains and lettered in three sports at Santa Fe High.

They had been sent to take out the Fidelista leader, Emiliano, but shortly after the convoy had dropped them off near the village of La Ciénega a few miles south of Santa Fe, things had started to go wrong. They were trudging across the flats toward their designated firing point in the hills when the Lieutenant called a halt to do some preventative maintenance on a blister that was suddenly developing inside one of his newly issued boots. Like all infantrymen, he understood the importance of taking good care of his feet, but on this occasion he forgot the most important rule of good foot care in the high deserts of New Mexico: always check your boots for bugs before you put them back on.

The consequence of his carelessness had been a painful sting from a fearsome looking scorpion that had kept him off his feet for the rest of the night and most of the next day. The foot had grown progressively worse, until now it was so swollen and discolored that Roberto had decided they were going to have to get some help.

The pain was making it difficult for the Lieutenant to concentrate on his target.

Forget the foot, he thought. Forget the damn mission. Forget everything except those crosshairs.

"Steady breeze quartering left to right, sir," reported the Corporal.

"I'm sighting on that nearest bunch near that big clump of yellow weeds."

"The rabbit bush. Yes sir." The Corporal checked his range finder. "That's about 580, sir. I'd give it about three inches for the wind."

The Lieutenant's brand new Viper still smelled of Cosmoline. It was an awesome weapon, designed to kill at incredible ranges–fifteen hundred yards and beyond–depending on which of the stories you believed. It was a fifty caliber, semi-automatic rifle with accuracy enough to hit a man or even a prairie dog at this distance, yet power enough to punch through an inch of armor plate if need be.

The crosshairs had finally stopped dancing back and forth across his target.

"Ready on the firing line," he said almost to himself.

Slowly he began to apply pressure to the trigger, letting out his breath at the same time. The crosshairs steadied, and for a moment he was back in Tennessee, hunting wood chucks with his dad. Instead of the Viper, he was using a little .222 Remington with a six-power scope. The big chuck was lazily eating a stem of Johnson grass on the far side of a pasture. The wind was gusting strongly directly across his line of fire, but he gave the windage his best guess and squeezed the trigger.

The shot came without warning as it should, and when he looked again, the whistle pig was lying on its side with one leg twitching spasmodically.

"Fine shot, Son!" said his dad, and the young Sandy McDowell had lived on that praise for weeks.

"SNAP!" The sound of the firing pin falling on an empty chamber ended his dream of Tennessee, but the crosshairs remained rock solid on target, and he knew that if this had been the real thing, the big bullet would have struck with shattering force, knocking his man head over heels, dead before he bounced. At least that is what he had been told.

"How do we score it, sir?"

"Ten ring," said the Lieutenant confidently.

"More like Maggie's Drawers, sir. Looked to me like you flinched."

Maggie's Drawers was the affectionate name given to the red flag waved by the shot spotters on the thousand yard range to signal a clean miss. The Lieutenant had not seen the red flag waved in front of one of his targets since he had competed as the youngest shooter in the Junior Big Bore Matches at Camp Perry, Ohio.

He was only fourteen and so nervous that it was a miracle he was flagged only once during the tournament . He returned to Knoxville with a bruised shoulder from the recoil of the big Winchester and a burning desire to compete at Camp Perry again. That was more than ten years ago, and since then he had learned to control those crosshairs and place his shots with deadly accuracy.

Roberto was proud to be teamed with the best marksman in the battalion, but right now he was more worried about what would if happen if a Fidelista patrol spotted them.

"Think you can make it to that little house up there on the ridge line?" he asked.

"With your help."

"You got it."

They stowed the Viper and the rest of their equipment in the packs they had brought with them.

"I'll come back for this later," said the Corporal, helping the Lieutenant to his feet.

"I feel like a damn fool putting us in this fix," said the Lieutenant.

"Just lean on me, sir," replied his friend. "One step at a time."

2

Tony Baca was enjoying the sunset. Tipped back in a chrome dinette chair beside his backdoor, he nursed a beer and watched the sun disappearing behind the peaks of the Jemez Mountains. It was like watching a tiger trying to conceal itself behind a pile of tumble weeds, he thought. No, better a jaguar. After all, hadn't his great grandfather killed a jaguar up near Las Trampas a long time ago? The big cat had made it all the way up from Mexico along the Rio Grande. Finding one this far north was a rare event, but that didn't matter to the ranchers. As soon as it started taking their sheep, they tracked it down and killed it. In those days people knew what to do about interlopers from south of the border, thought Tony.

Sheep country for his great grandfather, but what the Hell kind of a country was it for him?

To his left the last rays of the sun glimmered on the tailings of the old gold mine on the flank of the Ortiz Mountains. An open pit mine had operated there before the fighting began. Every few days they would blast away the over-burden, and the thump of the explosion would roll across Santa Fe, but no one complained because people were proud that they had their very own gold mine along with everything else the tourists came to see.

Then the Fidelistas arrived, bringing their violence and their terror, and the mine owners packed up and left Santa Fe for good, along with all of the tourists and most of the Anglos. Only the oldest families remained, some to join the Fidelistas, and some, like Tony and his wife Lupe, to wait for the violence to pass like some kind of terrible summer thunderstorm.

So now the mine was deserted. But the explosions hadn't stopped, thought Tony. There were still plenty of goddam explosions.

He stood up abruptly, chugged the last of his beer, and hurled the bottle down the slope behind his house. Somewhere in the brush it smashed against a rock with a satisfying crash, and Tony listened carefully to the silence that followed.

He heard only the voices of some neighbor kids playing down at the church. In the stillness he could almost make out what they were shouting. Sounds carried cleanly in the thin, desert air. At night he could hear the gunfire from a long way off, the crack of rifle fire and the sputter of automatic weapons erupting suddenly out of the stillness like sparks from a cedar log. At first, he had found a bizarre kind of entertainment in those distant skirmishes. It was better than the movies, he had told Lupe, and he would sit out after dark listening to the firefights and watching for the occasional streak of tracers or rockets.

But as the fighting wore on, the novelty wore off, and Tony began spending his evenings in the kitchen with Lupe, the two of them listening to the big radio when there was electricity or to the windup set when there wasn't. For more than a year now the newscasts from KOA in Denver or KOB in Albuquerque had been referring to areas of northern New Mexico and southern Colorado as "rebel held territory." They were full of bad news about Fidelista successes and the violence that seemed to be growing more common in the rest of the country, but Tony listened faithfully while Lupe tended to her sewing. It was something to do and safer than sitting outside, waiting to pick up a stray bullet.

This evening there was a reminder of why they called it "rebel held territory." Along the short stretch of old I-25 that the Bacas could see from their home in the village of La Ciénega, the wreck of a National Guard truck was sending a smudge of smoke across the luminous sky. This was a relic of the previous night's convoy, the victim of a land mine, he was sure. The explosion had awakened him and Lupe, and they had lain there, watching the faint glow of the flames on the vigas over their bed. Neither of them had bothered to get up and see what was happening. They knew. They knew too well. Always the army tried to keep the road open. Always the Fidelistas attacked them. It had been going on the same way for months. Tomorrow the truck would burn itself out, and the buzzards would begin work on what was left of the driver. By the time the buzzards were through, another convoy would come chugging up La Bajada Hill and there would be more explosions and more firefights.

So what else is new? he thought. There was nothing he could do about the Fidelistas except to try and stay out of their way. He and Lupe kept to themselves most of the time. They seldom went into Santa Fe, and when the Fidelistas made one of their rare visits to La Ciénega, the two of them did their best to stay out of sight. They called it their prairie dog strategy, staying close to their cozy den and diving for cover when danger came too close.

Tony took a last look around, searching the fading light for anything out of the ordinary. Most nights there was nothing of importance, but tonight he saw something that frightened him. Far down the slope two figures were moving slowly through the scrub brush. One man seemed to be helping the other walk so that they hobbled along in an awkward, three-legged sort of way. Tony watched just long enough to be sure they were headed in his direction. Then he picked up the dinette chair, carried it inside, and bolted the door behind him.

3

Unaware of the approaching strangers, two brothers were riding their bicycles in slow circles around the dusty yard of the little building that served the village of La Ciénega as a church. They had been keeping an eye on the deepening dusk, and it was time for them to head for home. They straddled their bikes and called to their friend.

"Father T.J.!"

"We got to go Father T.J. It's getting dark."

Father Triunfadór Jaramillo, O.S.A., appeared in the doorway of the chapel. He was a short man with a fierce black beard and gentle brown eyes. He wore an old fashioned habit cinched at his ample waist by a long leather strap that was the mark of the Augustinian order. The beard matched his rather bellicose name, but the gentle eyes told the real story of the priest who was known to all simply as Father T.J.

"Here's the ball," said the older boy, tossing a scruffy soccer ball to the priest. "Don't let anyone take it, will you?"

"I won't."

"It's the only one," said the younger boy, stating a fact that they all knew well enough.

"I will take good care of it," said the priest, thinking that the Church had always been a place of sanctuary, so why not for a soccer ball?

"Do you think you could get us another one?" said the older boy, without optimism.

"I can try."

"Maybe Emiliano would give you one," said the younger boy. "The Fidelistas have everything, no?"

"Shut up, estúpido!" laughed his brother. "You know that pendejo wouldn't give Father T.J. the sweat off his…"

"Maybe I could ask," interrupted the priest with a smile. "You watch how you talk, Joselito, and I will see if I can get a soccer ball."

He knew that the boy was right, of course. The Fidelistas would give him nothing but trouble even if he went begging to their leader. And besides, he didn't want Joselito and his little brother depending on them for anything. If there was to be a new soccer ball for La Ciénega, it would come from him and not from Emiliano and his henchmen.

"Tell your mother and sister I will enjoy the fry bread," said Father T.J.

"We have more, if you want," said the younger boy.

"This is enough for now," said the priest. "I might get fat."

They laughed at his joke. Everyone knew that Father T.J. was a priest who enjoyed his food, and the women of the village made sure he was always well supplied with the best tidbits from their kitchens.

"Tomorrow the catechism," said the priest seriously. "You come too, Ricardo."

The older boy popped a little wheelie with his bike. "Ricardo is joining the Fidelistas for a soccer ball. Aren't you, Bro?"

"Sure! You bet!" grinned Ricardo, making a dash toward the road. " Qué viva La Gente! The People Rule!"

The boys' laughter lifted Father T.J.'s spirits. Children were wonderful, he thought. They could laugh in the face of any catastrophe.

"God rules!" he called after them. "And don't you forget it!"

He watched the boys out of sight before hurrying back to the chapel. He would have to be quick if he wanted to visit Tony and Lupe before curfew.

True to his word, he carried the precious soccer ball back to his little bedroom behind the altar. There he collected his prayer book and the heavy, five-cell flashlight that he always carried when he went out after dark. For a moment he hefted it like a club and allowed himself to imagine how he might someday be forced to use it in self-defense. The thought made him so uncomfortable that he hurriedly crossed himself.

"Virgencita, forgive me," he breathed. As his penance, he broke the fry bread in half and wrapped one part in a napkin to give to the Bacas. It was only a short walk to their house on the edge of the village, but he had not called on them for a month. Tonight the fry bread would help him make up for that.

4

Lupe Baca looked up from her mending, surprised to see her husband carrying the old chair into her kitchen.

"Don't you bring that thing in here!" she said sharply.

Tony put the chair down and headed for the living room where he checked to make sure the front door was bolted.

"It's probably got spiders on it," insisted his wife when he returned.

"No spiders," said Tony.

"Well, why are you bringing such a mess into my kitchen?"

Tony sat down on the old chair as if to confirm its right to be there.

"I saw a couple of men down by the highway," he said.

"Doing what?"

"Heading this way."

There was a moment of silence as she considered the news. She understood now why Tony had brought the chair inside. A heavy chair could be used to batter down a door ... or worse.

"Could you tell who they were?"

"No."

Tony saw an uncharacteristic moment of fear in her eyes.

"Fidelistas?" she asked.

"I doubt it."

"Guns?"

"I couldn't tell."

Lupe picked up her mending. She did not want to think of the two men approaching her little home in the dusk.

"The electricity is on," she said, pointing to her sewing lamp.

"So maybe now it will rain," said Tony. It was their joke that the electricity had become as unpredictable as the rain. Now on. Now off. Now here. Now there. And sometimes absent for a long, long time.

"At least you can charge up the battery," she said, still avoiding the two men coming up the slope toward them.

"Yes," said Tony. "And I think I will clean the guns also."

He went to the closet and connected the trickle charger to the old car battery they used for emergencies. Then he took out a single shot 12 gauge shotgun and a bolt action .22 rifle. He put the ammunition on the kitchen table and began rubbing the rifle with an oily rag.

"I remember my father with these guns," he said.

"We used to shoot the shotgun only on the Fourth of July and Cinco de Mayo," said Lupe.

"And New Year's Eve."

"Now there are no more holidays."

"There's Fiesta."

"Fiesta," said Lupe disgustedly. "If you want to associate with a bunch of drunken Fidelistas. No one goes any more except for the drunks and a few crazy teenagers."

Tony began to load the .22. He remembered when Lupe herself was a teenager. She was so beautiful that it made his heart ache to think about it. No one could believe that a prize like Lupe was actually going steady with a goof ball like him, Tony-no-Baloney, and it made him very proud to see how jealous his friends were.

"This reminds me of when they blew up the prison," he said, thinking of the last time he had loaded that rifle.

Shortly after the Fidelistas had arrived in the area, Emiliano had blown two huge holes in the walls of the state penitentiary, allowing many convicts to escape. Some had joined the Fidelistas on the spot, but those who didn't tried to avoid the hundreds of State Police and National Guard troops who were searching for them by hiding out in the homes of local residents. Criminals roamed the area, looking for shelter, food, and a way out. Sometimes they simply took people hostage. Other times they did worse than that, and so for weeks the citizens of La Ciénega had gone about their lives armed to the teeth like characters in a Western movie.

"Be sure those are the hollow points," she said. "I think I hear something."

There was a definite sound of footsteps at the back door followed by a knock that sounded very loud in the little kitchen.

"Give me that thing and you go see who it is," said Lupe.

She took the rifle and shoved home a shell. Tony stood to one side as he worked the lock so his wife would have a clear shot. Then he turned off the lights and opened the door.

5

The two men who had been laboring through the half-light were within a hundred yards of the Baca's little adobe when they saw the porch lights go out. The Lieutenant sank to the ground, taking the weight off his swollen foot.

"Watch out you don't go sitting on a cactus," said the Corporal, dryly.

"Does everything up here either stick you or sting you?" groaned the Lieutenant. He felt very much like a green horn in this barren land of rocks and thorns. Nothing here bore the slightest resemblance to anything he was used to back home in Tennessee.

He had spent his high school years at a military school near Nashville and from there he had gone straight to Ft. Bragg. Now, six years later he had emerged from his training as a Special Forces sniper, First Lieutenant Sanford McDowell, a man on a mission which was now in jeopardy because of his own carelessness.

McDowell reached down and touched his foot gingerly. The swelling was getting worse, and it occurred to him that his foot might actually split open. He put that thought aside and tried to focus on the business at hand.

"What's going on over there?" he whispered.

The Corporal had been studying the little house with a pair of night glasses. "They've got a visitor," he said. "But don't worry. It's someone I know. A priest."

"So at least I get a decent burial."

"Real men don't die from no piddling little scorpion sting," said Chavez. But they do get pretty sick sometimes, he thought, and Lupe Baca was just the person to take care of that ugly looking foot before it got any worse.

"You sure about these people?" asked McDowell.

"This guy is my cousin," said Chavez. "I've known him since we were kids. I'd trust him with my life."

"That's what you are doing," said the Lieutenant. "One word to the Fidelistas and we're dead meat."

"Have faith in your trusty guide," said the Corporal, thinking to himself how this was all like some sort of crazy rerun of a cowboy movie. Long ago, the Army had pacified the West with the help of local scouts who knew the lay of the land. Now history was repeating itself with the Fidelistas playing a sort of Keystone Cops version of the Apaches to their U.S Cavalry. Thank God Emiliano was no Geronimo or things might have gotten even worse.

He handed his binoculars to the Lieutenant.

"When you see me wave, show a light so I can come back and get you."

"And if I don't see you wave?"

"Then hunker down and wait."

Chavez headed off through the scrub, angling toward the little house. Moonrise would be in about an hour, he thought. With Tony's help, he might be able to retrieve the big pack they had left behind and return before midnight. In the meantime, maybe Lupe could work one of her miracles on that foot.

He began calling out as he approached the little house. It was not a good idea to go creeping up on folks after dark these days.

"Hey, Tony! It's me, Roberto."

The porch light went on, and the door opened a crack. "Roberto?"

"The one and only."

The door opened wide, and the Corporal could see his cousin standing to one side with his wife behind him leveling a .22 rifle in his general direction.

"Roberto?" said Tony. "What are you doing back up here?"

"It's a long story, Bro. Let me in and I'll tell you all about it."

There was a pause, as Lupe conferred with her husband. When Tony spoke again, he sounded more like the man that Roberto had known all his life, Tony-no-Baloney, his old compadre.

"Come on in, amigo. Father T.J. is here too."

Roberto crossed the yard and slipped through the door. Lupe was still standing in the kitchen with the rifle cradled in her arms, searching the darkness for trouble.

6

Emiliano had awakened just in time to watch Truchas Peak turn the color of watermelon flesh in the last light of day. It happened this way only rarely, and Emiliano was pleased to see the blush of the sunset on the mountain one more time before he started on his journey north. It might be many days before he saw Truchas Peak again, and there was always a chance that it would be much longer than that.

Still, it would be good to get away for a while. He was growing weary of the vampire life he led, sleeping most of the day and arising only at dusk to conduct the stealthy business of the Fidelistas. Like a vampire, Emiliano lived in a remote, mountain stronghold guarded by his henchmen, and like a vampire, he could be very dangerous.

Just now, Emiliano did not look so dangerous as he searched for his underwear among the rumpled sheets. Nor did he feel very dangerous, having spent a long siesta in the company of Tina Roybal, one of his more exuberant girlfriends.

Tina was a plump little radio operator from Taos. She had two younger sisters that Emiliano also coveted, and because of her special status as both radio operator and official girlfriend, she had arranged a private, going-away party for him that afternoon in his quarters.

A bottle of rum and some commendable signs of initiative on Tina's part had made the afternoon a definite success. Emiliano had partaken himself of her favors more than usual, and as he finished dressing, he was beginning to think that the interlude might have really been too much of a good thing.

As usual, Tina had departed while he slept, taking the rest of the rum and a few of his cigars. (A special treat for her grandmother, she always said.) But he was not sorry that she was gone. His thoughts were too full of the journey he was about to take to be distracted by anything as transitory as a woman.

Two weeks before, he had received word that Boss Beckwith was coming to Creed, Colorado. Boss Beckwith himself, the commander of the Patriots, would be inspecting his southernmost base for a week. After much thought and not a little rum, Emiliano had decided to seize the opportunity and make the trip to Creed to meet his opposite number face to face. Mano a mano you could say. Just the two of them to talk. To talk what? Strategy? Weapons? An alliance? Politically, the Patriots and the Fidelistas were opposites, but if they could form some sort of temporary alliance they might at least make some progress against the holdouts in Ratón.

It would be Emiliano's first journey into unfamiliar territory since he had been plucked from the ranks of the young Zapatistas in Mexico and sent to Cuba for further training. Emiliano never knew who his patron was, but someone must have detected in him the ruthlessness, the ambition and the charisma that made him a leader. All Emiliano knew was that one day he was given a suitcase full of ill-fitting clothes, an airplane ticket to Havana, and instructions to pay attention to everything he was taught.

He had done just that, despite all the distractions that the Cuban women had to offer. After a few weeks of preliminary training he had graduated to terrorist school where he spent three more months learning how to make the bombs and booby traps that would kill or maim great numbers of innocent people. His instructors were Asians–Chinese he had guessed–who spoke little Spanish. Only an instruction manual, some videotapes, and an incredibly blonde interpreter named Kirsten had gotten him through the course.

The part about explosives, he had learned particularly well. Just how well, he had demonstrated shortly after returning home by blowing up an armored BMW along with two Pemex executives and their girlfriends.

Even then, and for a long time after, he was only a tiny cog in the vast machinery of international terrorism. But then he found success in his own little piece of what he liked to call the Reconquest of America. Soon he became known as Emiliano of the raid on Los Alamos, Emiliano of the car bombs, and Emiliano of the political assassinations. Now he was a man among men, a revolutionary among revolutionaries, and the leader of a guerilla force that seemed capable of keeping the entire U.S. Army at bay.

And so he would go to Creed and forge an alliance with Beckwith and his Patriots. It was time to strike and strike hard. Soon much of the American Southwest would be returned to the control of the People's Republic of Mexico. He wanted to have a large and prominent role in making that happen, and a brief alliance with Beckwith was just the thing to help bring it about.

Filled with these heady thoughts, Emiliano flicked on the lamp next to his shaving mirror and examined his reflection. Naturally, he liked what he saw, finding only a few unruly hairs in his beard and a mustache that needed clipping.

A few snips with the scissors and a splash of cologne revived him completely, and he strode into the compound wearing his best fatigue jacket, his newest boots and a fresh cigar.

Nearby, several men sat at a plank table playing dominos.

"I want to see Alejandro and Peligro in the command post right away," he said to no one in particular. Men scurried to see that his orders were carried out, and Emiliano strode on toward the bunker, trailing a self-satisfied plume of cigar smoke.

7

Dalton Lamar Beckwith, Boss Beckwith to all but his oldest friends who called him Dalton Lamar in the Southern style, was enjoying his first plane ride in a long time. The old turbo prop was crowded with passengers making the most of their first chance to fly since his Patriots had proclaimed the region a "no fly zone" several months before. As soon as the warning was announced, all civilian air traffic had been grounded. Nothing had flown, except military aircraft. But now, his point made and with the long trip to Creed in the planning stages, Beckwith had announced the cancellation of the no fly zone, and within a short time the airlines were back at full operation.

Beckwith had a strong military background. A hero of the abortive Balkans Campaign and the disastrous retreat from Belgrade, he had gone on to become a major in the Colorado National Guard. Then came a job as a late night talk show host on radio station KOA. That fifty thousand-watt powerhouse carried his deeply resonant and nearly hypnotic voice to hundreds of thousands of dedicated fans. Night after night he proclaimed his common sense conservatism and unabashed patriotism to all who would listen, and from there it was only a short step to becoming the leader of the Patriots, a powerful, paramilitary organization that was now in virtual control of most of the Rocky Mountain states.

He had booked one of the first available flights to Colorado Springs under an assumed name and, with his usual panache, strolled right through the Pocatello airport without being noticed. For a disguise he had worn some vaguely South American glasses that gave him a Brazilian look. The effect was aided by the fact that no one who saw him would ever match the famous voice of Boss Beckwith with the foreign looking little man clutching a plastic sack full of fruit. Like many radio personalities, Beckwith's voice did not give any clue to his physical appearance, and oddly enough, few of his photos had ever been distributed by the authorities.

It was just as he had told his men; if you didn't push their terrorist profile hot buttons, you could pretty much go where you wanted. Sure enough, at the crucial moment when he had passed through the boarding gate, none of the security guards had given him a second glance.

He wouldn't stand for such carelessness from his own people, of course. Those security folks at Pocatello should have been more alert. No wonder his Patriots were making such progress against the Statists, the party of politicians and feckless do-gooders who had been busily feathering their nests for decades. So much of the country now operated in a kind of slack-jawed, third world sort of way, he thought. Even the U.S. military seemed hardly a match for the highly motivated men and women who had joined the Patriots in the hope of restoring the country to its former glory. Still, he could hardly believe that his Patriots had so far been able to win a protracted stalemate in their confrontation with the armed forces of the United States.

In the distance Beckwith could barely make out the glow of Denver, illuminating the perpetual smog that choked the city. The little turbo-prop was giving it a wide birth because Denver air space was still closed to all traffic except transcontinental flights. The authorities felt that by constantly patrolling within a ten-mile radius around the airport and mandating a steep approach for the big jets, they could minimize the chance of having one blasted out of the sky.

No plane was ever attacked, of course, but not because of those elaborate defense measures. Rather it was because the Patriots had never intended to shoot down any planes to begin with. For Beckwith, the threat had been nothing but a bluff. It was victory enough that a word from him had managed to tie up air travel across a wide part of the West and had kept hundreds of men busy guarding an airport that never really needed guarding.

He had raised the Statists with a busted flush and they had folded. He had won all the chips, and the chips meant power. If people believed you were powerful, you were. If they didn't, you weren't. It was as simple as that, and after the resounding success of his little "no fly" scam, Boss Beckwith imagined that he was very powerful indeed.

8

Meanwhile, three truly powerful men were just concluding their meal with a round of Stilton cheese and Madeira in the private dining room of one of Washington D.C.'s most exclusive clubs. They would have been very pleased to know about Boss Beckwith's delusion of power because they had played a large part in giving it to him.

These men traded in delusions, and it had been their idea all along to make the Patriots appear more powerful than they actually were. They had done the same thing for Emiliano and the Fidelistas, portraying him as some sort of military genius leading a band of hardened guerillas which might someday leave the protection of their mountain stronghold and spread death and destruction across all of Arizona and Southern California.

These three men, with their Havana cigars and their fine old Madeira, represented corporations that controlled over eighty percent of America's television networks, radio stations, newspapers, and magazines. They could dictate the content of virtually all the media except for the Internet, and they were working on that.

In a way, they were inventors. Day by day, week by week, they invented the America that they wanted the public to perceive. They decided what was to be known and what was not to be known, who was to be believed and who was not to be believed. They decided what people should be concerned about and what they should ignore. It was not so much that these men created events, but rather that they shaped them to fit their purposes. It seemed a small thing to be able to do, yet it gave them almost complete control over the entire country.

For now and for a long time their purpose had been to further the interests of the Statists in general and of this President in particular. It was to this end that they had come to the nation's capitol. The last trap was about to be sprung, and they wanted to be in for the kill.

9

*P*ATRIOT RADIO IS ON THE AIR…

This is Colonel Dalton Lamar Beckwith of the Patriots speaking to you from somewhere in the Rockies. Today I want to remind you why we are resisting the Statist regime.

In the first place we have endured thirty years of Statist administrations. They have tried to hold onto their power anyway they could. The have pitted race against race, class against class and even gender against gender in an effort to win your votes. They have lied to you shamelessly trying to conceal the fact that their policies are ruining America.

Our standard of living has fallen year after year. Our educational system is in crisis. We are threatened by violent crime on a massive scale. Riots are breaking out in our major cities, and the labor unions are resorting more and more to hoodlum tactics to extort higher and higher wages from their employers.

Even so, the Statists continue to believe that they are right. Even in the face of massive evidence to the contrary, they cling to the fanatical belief that the policies of the left are the only acceptable course of action for our country. They believe that their answers to the problems of this nation are the only answers. Therefore, they believe that they must hold on to the Presidency at all costs.

Like all budding tyrants they have convinced themselves that the end justifies the means, and that they have a right to cheat, steal, lie, or even kill to win an election. They have raised illegal campaign funds, bussed illegal voters to the poles, and even stuffed ballot boxes to win some elections.

Worst of all, the media have been demonstrating their liberal bias by acting as apologists for these scoundrels, refusing to investigate the crimes of the Statists and focusing on less important things such as murder trails and sex scandals, instead. It is the same trick used by the Roman emperors. They gave the people bread and circuses in hopes of distracting them from the very real problems that eventually led to the fall of Rome itself.

Through the use of these tactics, the Statists have managed to stay in power well into the twenty-first century. They have stayed in power for so long and by some unfair means that those of us on the right have given up hope of defeating them in a fair fight at the ballot box. We believe that the only way to restore the old balance between left and right in American politics is to drive these rascals out of power and return to the honest contest between political philosophies that used to invigorate this country. This country needs a fresh start, and we intend to give America a chance at that fresh start, even if we have to use force to do it.

Imagine, if you will, two old men who have played checkers with each other every day for years. For a long time, the contest is even. Each player wins as often as he loses. At first they are friendly competitors. They follow the rules of the game. But then one of them begins to cheat. He cheats so often and so boldly that his opponent soon realizes that there is no longer any point in playing the game at all and kicks over the checkerboard scattering the checkers far and wide.

And that is what we are doing, my friends. We are kicking over the checkerboard and demanding a new game without cheating. Our goal is to restore honest elections of the type that made this country great. If we fail, then we will simply be taken over by the same giant police state that threatens to overwhelm us now. But, my friends, if we succeed, we can save America. We are up against a powerful opponent, one that will stop at nothing, but we will fight for our freedom rather than submit to the slow suffocation of rule by the Statists and their accomplices.

These are dangerous times we live in, my friends. Are you prepared to join us and dedicate your life to saving our Constitution? Or are you simply going to sit back in your TV lounger and let the Statists enslave you? If you want a free America where the contest of ideas can be played out fairly, then I urge you to join us here in the still unconquered West.

10

Roberto and Tony ventured out to retrieve the Lieutenant's big rifle and the rest of the equipment shortly after moonrise. In the clear night air, the features of the broad landscape stood out cleanly, black on black against the stars. Fifty miles to the south was the Sandia Mountain, thrusting out of the desert floor near Albuquerque. Much closer, and in the opposite direction, was the Santa Fe Mountain; while to the west the lights of Los Alamos festooned the foothills of the Jemez range. These mountains were really the remains of a long dead volcano, which had produced the gigantic lava flow, which now formed the very ground on which they stood. The lava flow was hundreds of feet thick and ended in the steep escarpment known as La Bajada Hill, invisible in the middle distance between where they stood and Albuquerque, nearly two thousand feet nearer to sea level.

Moving slowly and keeping a sharp eye out for Fidelista patrols, the two friends had returned just before midnight lugging the heavy pack between them.

"What you got in here?" asked Tony. "Atomic bombs?"

"Just ammo and stuff," replied Roberto.

"Stuff that could get me killed," he said gruffly.

"What's wrong, Bro? You sound kind of touchy."

"Why shouldn't I be touchy? First you show up at my back door with some skinny Anglo who's got a foot the size of a cantaloupe, and now you've got me running around the countryside after curfew. We could get shot, you know."

The back door opened a crack, and Lupe looked out, still clutching the little .22 rifle.

"You two quit talking and get in here," she hissed. "It's way after curfew."

Inside, the Lieutenant was stretched out on the living room couch, listening to Tony's big radio with the earphones, while next to him Father T.J. dozed in an old recliner. Lupe had turned out most of the lights so they could get some rest. The curtains were drawn tight giving the room a cozy feeling despite the institutional tone of the linoleum floors, which were softened only by a few hooked rugs. The furniture was sparse and simple. Beside the big naugahyde couch and Father T.J.'s recliner, the room held only a couple of straight chairs, a nondescript coffee table, a small book shelf full of paperbacks, and a shrine to the Virgin of Guadalupe complete with votive candles and a small plaster statue of the Madonna.

Similar shrines and furnishings could be found in Spanish homes all over northern New Mexico, for the real Santa Fe Style was not what the tourists had come to see, but rather something quite humble and unpretentious like the people whose lives it reflected.

Lupe set two steaming cups of coffee on the kitchen table and the men headed straight for them without being told.

"How is that foot?" asked Roberto nodding toward the living room.

"Not too good. He needs to give it a rest."

"How much rest?" asked Tony.

"Two or three days."

"Isn't there anything you can do to help?"

"Maybe if I had the right ingredients I could brew something up," she said seriously.

Tony knew that she was talking about the medicinal herbs that her grandmother, a famous curandera, had taught her to use.

"I thought we had some of that stuff stashed away," he said.

"Not the right things, mi vida. But there used to be that little shop in Santa Fe. We could go see if they had anything left."

"I thought you were staying away from Fiesta."

"We are going in before Fiesta even starts, mi amor. We're going to find help for our new friend here. Anyway, if we have to go in town, that would be the perfect time. Tomorrow night is the burning of Zozobra. Everyone will be drunk.' You could ride an elephant through town and no one would notice."

"She's right," said Roberto. "You know how Fiesta is."

"There, you see?" said Lupe. Maybe Father T.J. will loan us his beloved Esmeralda, so we can drive into town and get out quickly."

"That old van may not even be in driving condition," said Tony, knowing that, even if this was true, little he could say would deflect his wife from her purpose once she had decided on a course of action. The little Chevy van had been a familiar sight around the village of La Ciénega for years. Sometimes on a mission of mercy, sometimes carrying elderly parishioners into town to shop, Esmeralda had served the community well. Lately, however, Father T.J. had driven her only rarely as tires and gasoline became harder and harder to find. As far as Tony knew, Esmeralda had not been driven for at least six months.

"Tony, mi amor," coaxed Lupe, "I believe this is the right thing for us to do, and if it is, then God will provide."

After that he said no more, but in his heart Tony felt certain that if going into Santa Fe was the right thing to do, it might also prove to be the first step in a chain of events that would completely disrupt their quiet lives in La Ciénega.

11

Boss Beckwith's powerful message was followed by a program reviewing highpoints of American history and news reports that had not been broadcast by the major networks such as CCN. Then the station went off the air with the playing of the "National Anthem," and Lieutenant McDowell removed his earphones. It had been a long time since he had heard the old anthem and suddenly his imagination was filled with the sights and sounds of the American Legion ballpark near his home in Knoxville. He was standing in center field with his baseball cap held over his heart while a scratchy recording of the "National Anthem" blared out over the PA system. He could hear the flag flapping in the breeze above his head and the rattle of the ropes against the steel flagpole. He knew that his dad was standing at attention somewhere in the bleachers behind him saluting that flag, so he did the same, not moving to shoo away the gnats that hovered near his face or ostentatiously spitting in the grass like his teammates.

His girlfriend Bonnie had come to watch him play too. She was his special girl throughout his last two years of military school, a fundamentalist preacher's daughter who carried a small edition of the New Testament in her purse instead of a compact. They went everywhere together, she to his baseball games and shooting matches and he to her father's church on Sunday mornings and Wednesday evenings. The relationship was good for them both, but it was not strong enough to overcome his determination to follow a military career. Although she might have liked the uniform, she wanted nothing to do with the life of an army wife. Living in the South, where so many military bases were located, she had seen enough long separations and broken marriages to know that such a life was not for her. Sandy McDowell understood, and knew that she must be right, but still her slender face and the soft touch of her hand came back to him from time to time in his daydreams.

The "National Anthem" came to an end. Lately it had become fashionable to substitute "America the Beautiful" for the old anthem on the grounds that its lyrics were less warlike. Sandy McDowell thought the substitution was ludicrous. He knew that those lines about rockets and bombs were all about a young democracy battling against a tyrant who was trying to put an end to the pernicious idea of rule by the people. He had grown up reading about men whose lives were lessons in gallantry and devotion to duty. As a cadet he had survived the rigors of hazing and the stress of all night marches by remembering the example of those men.

Now, as he lay on Tony Baca's couch with his swollen foot resting on a cushion he faced the likelihood that his first real mission with Special Forces would end in failure, and for the life of him, he could not recall a single story that would give him consolation before he slept.

12

Emiliano's command post was a well-fortified bunker. The fresh cut vigas which formed the low ceiling gave a piney scent to the air, while the single lantern that hung from the center beam, added the smell of kerosene to a haze of cigar smoke. This windowless little room was the center of Emiliano's world and the place where he kept his favorite toys. One corner was crowded with short wave radio equipment, while the workbench where he manufactured the bombs that had made him famous occupied another wall. Above the workbench were gun racks filled with assault rifles, while in the center of the room was a table covered with maps and the remains of that morning's breakfast. Emiliano was just beginning to look for a snack among the leftovers, when Alejandro and Peligro arrived.

"You wanted to see us, Jefe?" said Alejandro.

They both knew what he was about to say. Nothing was really secret if Tina Roybal knew about it, and rumors had been circulating for days about Emiliano's trip to Creed. Nevertheless, they listened gravely while he spelled out his plans and assigned them their duties.

To Alejandro, he gave the task of moving the men to their winter quarters at the old Sikh compound near Española , and to Peligro, he gave the job of driving him to Creed and acting as his bodyguard along the way.

Peligro had come up from Mexico with Emiliano. The two were like brothers, and Emiliano wanted the comfort of having the little Nicaraguan with him while he was so far from the security of his bunker. Peligro had been fighting the United States and its various surrogates since he was a child. He was a dark little man with a fierce Mayan face, a remorseless killer who was known to be absolutely fearless. Best of all, both his bravery and his good luck had been proven beyond doubt in any number of battles with the Yankees.

Alejandro was less of a warrior than he was a crusader. He had been born in the nearby village of Peñasco and had joined the Fidelistas more out of a wish to settle old wrongs than a desire to commit new ones.

A thin European face and a sharply chiseled nose were clear evidence that he was descended from a young Spanish nobleman, who had marched north with Captain General DeVargas to reclaim Santa Fe after the Pueblo Revolt. For his bravery the young trooper had been given a grant of land by the king of Spain himself, and for more than two centuries the Vigils had held claim to thousands of acres along the high road to Taos.

Then came the American occupation and hard times for his family. Before long, the lawyers and politicians had taken nearly everything they owned and the famous Vigil Grant was nothing more than a worthless sheet of parchment locked away in an old strong box. Within a single generation, Alejandro's patrimony had been whittled down to nothing but a few small farms and the rights to a little water from the old acequias near Peñasco.

Alejandro grew up learning a family history which was full of tales about how the Yankees had swindled the Vigils, and when the Fidelistas had begun recruiting among his friends and neighbors, he had joined at once, hoping to regain the lands that were rightfully his.

Emiliano knew these two men well, but while he may have understood their motivations, he did not share their goals. Emiliano was neither a killer nor a crusader. He was simply a leader. He told others what to do, and they did it. It was easy for him because he was a natural actor who knew how to play to his audience.

He was also a bit of a thief.

When he and his men breached the walls of the state prison with their explosives, one of the escapees was a career safe cracker. This unfortunate man stayed with Emiliano long enough to show him how to loot the exclusive vacation homes of the rich and famous that were tucked away in the hills around Santa Fe. For weeks the two searched out these abandoned hideaways, located their wall safes and blew them open with bits of Emiliano's favorite explosive, Symtex. In this way they accumulated an impressive collection of jewelry that had been left behind by homeowners who had not bothered to come back and collect it after the troubles began. But the little safe cracker saved the best for last.

The Museum of New Mexico possessed a huge collection of Navajo, Zuni, and Hopi jewelry. This trove of squash blossom necklaces, turquoise bracelets and rings, plus elaborate concho belts was stored for safe keeping in a vault beneath the Museum of Native American Art. Plundering this treasure would be more than a two-man job, so Emiliano enlisted the help of his two lieutenants for this final caper.

The four men slipped quietly into Santa Fe one night, broke into the basement of the museum, blew open the vault, and carted away several hundred pounds of antique silver jewelry. They dumped this loot into a sturdy crate along with the rest of the treasure that Emiliano and the safe cracker had been gathering and hauled the whole thing to Shidoni, an abandoned sculpture garden a few miles north of town.

Here, between the huge statue of a grotesquely elongated giraffe and a Native American earth mother, they began digging. They kept at it until they had dug a hole, which seemed a little bigger than was actually needed for the crate. The safe cracker put down his shovel and was about to register a complaint about the extra digging when Emiliano signaled to Peligro, who stepped quickly behind the little convict, and with a deft stroke of his knife, cut the poor man's throat all the way to the spine. Emiliano shoved the dying man into the hole, and stood back while his two faithful lieutenants gently lowered the crate down beside the body and covered them both with dirt.

After that, only Peligro and Alejandro knew about the location of his secret treasure, and Emiliano made sure to keep them close, where he could keep a constant watch on their loyalty.

"Fiesta begins tomorrow night," he said to them both.

The two men nodded, knowing what was coming next.

"We are going of course," said Emiliano.

Peligro smiled. There were always fights at Fiesta.

"All except you, Alejandro. You will stay behind with a few men to make sure the camp is secure."

"Sí, Jefe," said Alejandro.

"And you, Peligro," said Emiliano with a sharp look into the killer eyes. "No fighting. This is for propaganda." Emiliano carefully stubbed out his cigar, letting the words sink in. "Everyone is to put on his best uniform," he said at last. "We will carry side arms, but no rifles. We don't need to look like a bunch of banditos."

Emiliano had decided to make a short speech before the burning of Zozobra. He would simply walk out on stage and say a few words to the people. He had a right to speak to them, especially since he now represented the only authority in the region. The U.S. Army was hiding in Albuquerque, and the legislators had fled the capitol. He had assassinated the mayor and murdered most of the city's police. He knew that he was not popular with the people, but at least they must respect him. They must be convinced that he was in complete control.

Which brought him to the part of his plan which he especially liked.

"Peligro," he said. "I am going to speak to the people tonight."

"Sí, Jefe."

"There will be many beautiful young girls there."

Peligro smiled again. This was getting better and better.

"Some will be drunk, some will be willing, and some will need persuasion. I don't care which type you choose as long as she is very young and very beautiful. Bring her to me while I am speaking. Bring her right up on the stage so everyone can see her. They should see that we can take anyone we want."

Peligro nodded

"Later, she will go with us to Creed as a gift for El Señor Beckwith."

"Young and beautiful," repeated Peligro.

"Very young and very thin. I am tired for awhile of gorditas."

"Sí, Jefe. No more Tina Roybals."

The two men laughed.

"And no bruises either, my friend," warned Emiliano. "Señor Beckwith is an important man. I don't want to offend him by offering him damaged goods."

13

"Mr. President."

The old man looked up, half-startled. Odd that they still called him that after all these years.

"What is it, Norton?"

"I need you to sign these, sir."

He cleared a spot on his desk and signed the authorizations without reading them. They meant that he would also be on the hook for the attack if things went sour. But, so what? You always had to have someone to blame, and the truth was that he didn't have much choice in the matter. He had been under virtual house arrest for over a year now.

A lot of innocent people would probably die tomorrow night, he thought. But that was politics. What did a few people matter compared to the prize that was at stake. They were going for the big one and for that, the end justified just about any means. And what was wrong with that? Only losers had to explain.

For just a moment he thought of all the other casualties of that particular philosophy. It was a long list to be sure, but certain things just had to be done. Had to be done! No choice! No one's fault, really. Certainly not his. If people got in the way, they got crushed. And only fools got in the way.

He turned and looked out the window. Beyond the first lighted fairway there was nothing but darkness, but he had just about had his fill of the damn view anyway. In fact he had had his fill of everything down here in Arkansas. He was ready to get back to D.C.

"What is it the military calls civilian casualties, Norton?"

"Collateral damage, sir."

"Right. Well, we'll probably have a fair amount of collateral damage tomorrow night. Are our network folks on top of things?"

"I expect so, sir."

"Just think, Norton. What would we have done all these years without a little help from our friends in the media? We'd have been out of business decades ago."

"Yes, sir."

"Misdirection, Norton. That's the ticket. As long as they're looking the other way, you can get away with any damn thing you please."

Norton liked the old man. He admired the way he could look you straight in the eye and tell you the biggest lie under the sun with a straight face.

"We'll see, sir," he said. "This one may be stretching things a bit though."

"Let them scream all they want. Anyway, we're blaming this one on those Patriot jerks."

Norton edged toward the door. He could see the old man wanted to talk, and if he didn't break away soon he might be here for half an hour.

"What's this I hear about them canceling their no-fly zone? Is that true or is it just a rumor?"

"Far as we can tell it's the real thing, sir. Rotten luck, really."

"How can it be a real emergency if the goddam planes are flying again?"

"That's why they're counting on you, sir."

The old man laughed. For a moment some of his old boyish charm showed through and played across his wrinkled features like sunshine.

"Damn straight! I can sell it. I can sell anything! I can sell goddam refrigerators to fucking Eskimos if I want. We'll use the same old line. It's all being done for the children! For the safety of our homes and families! For America, by God!"

The last bit sent him into whoops of laughter. After he had recovered himself he tried out a few time-tested lines, studying his performance in the mirror. As he warmed to his task he could almost feel the audience falling under his spell, but when he turned around to see how his own audience of one was enjoying the show, he was quite surprised to find himself quite alone. Norton had made good his escape.

14

The Statist Party had ruled the nation for the past quarter of a century, but they had never felt truly at ease with the historical monuments that graced its capitol. Deep in their hearts the Statists did not trust the lessons of history, and so they had no wish to encourage people to visit monuments which glorified the past. They preferred instead to focus everyone's attention on the promise of a prosperous future, which they claimed awaited everyone who would follow their rules and pay their taxes.

Over the years, they had closed down some of Washington D.C.'s most famous museums and monuments and cut back on maintenance of the rest. The academics at the Smithsonian Institution had taken the lead in this physical deconstruction of the nation's history. They had stored away the Wright Brothers biplane and the Spirit of St. Louis. They had packed up the relics of war and hidden away examples of the early inventions of Thomas Edison and Alexander Graham Bell. What history remained on display had been rewritten to suit their distorted view of this country's past.

They also campaigned to bring the monuments in line with their revisionist views. They closed down Arlington Cemetery and the Vietnam War Memorial on the grounds that they were far too militaristic. They renamed the memorials to Washington, Jefferson, Lincoln, and Roosevelt, referring to them only as "The Presidents' Monuments," and limiting the days on which they could be visited to Monday, Wednesday and Friday. Since Jefferson had been a slave owner, they removed his heroic statue from his monument, melted it down and recast it as an equally heroic statue of Eleanor Roosevelt, who had never owned any slaves and whose views they much preferred.

Finally, they arranged that the monuments should no longer be illuminated after dark, claiming that this would save energy and limit the creation of greenhouse gases. Only the White House remained lit by floodlights, for security purposes, it was alleged, and there it sat on this particular night, shining brightly in the darkness like some gigantic, white marble, Moby Dick, adrift on a sea of ignorance, in search of an Ahab to do battle with.

The White House was open for business twenty-four hours a day, and it was to one of the tiny communications offices buried deep in its belly that a FAX of the document the former President had signed was directed. A sleepy clerk slipped the message straight into a heavy manila envelope marked "Eyes Only," and included it with a batch of dispatches which would be delivered to the President, early the next morning.

FRIDAY
SEPTEMBER TENTH

15

Each year the Santa Fe Fiesta opened with the burning of Zozobra, a modern day scapegoat, also known as Old Man Gloom, who personified the worries and troubles of all Santa Feans. His ritual sacrifice at the beginning of each year's Fiesta was said to free the people from those cares and to liberate them so that they could properly celebrate Fiesta.

This barbaric spectacle had not always been a part of the celebration, which had been established in 1684 to commemorate the reconquest of Santa Fe by Captain General Diego DeVargas. In those days there had been no Zozobra at all. Old Man Gloom did not put in an appearance until the 1920's when he was dreamed up out of thin air by a committee of civic boosters who hoped to enliven their time worn little celebration with enough pagan and orgiastic overtones to really attract the tourists.

What might have seemed too gruesome a spectacle for most cities to stomach had been an instant success in Santa Fe. Zozobra quickly become the star of the show, and the tourists began crowding into Santa Fe each September to cheer his demise and enjoy the best three-day party west of the Mississippi. Since then, Old Man Gloom had grown larger and more lifelike, acquiring a voice and movable arms plus a belly full of fireworks to make his final moments truly spectacular.

It was an honor to be part of the crew who assembled the huge mannequin each year. Zozobra's creators were as proud of their role in the celebration as the Fiesta princesses who paraded before the crowds in their beautiful long gowns, or the handsome young men who escorted them across the stage, wearing the breast plates, helmets and swords of sixteenth century Spanish conquistadors.

With the coming of the Fidelistas and the closing of the local Sears store, the assemblers had to scrounge for materials to construct the giant effigy. Waste paper and paint were needed for the head, old sheets for the body, and plenty of combustible trash for the bonfire. Only the gunpowder and explosives were easy to get. The residue of war provided all they needed.

Several days before Fiesta, they began crafting Zozobra's huge papier maché head, complete with fearsome scowl and wild, glaring eyes. They hoisted this to the top of the telephone pole, which had been erected at the rear of the stage, and below it they nailed a crosspiece for the monster's shoulders. Here they attached the spidery, articulated arms and draped a huge piece of cloth stitched together from bed sheets to form the body. Finally they stuffed the whole thing with kindling and fireworks and hooked up the sound system to provide a proper voice for the monster's final agonies.

When the pyre was torched and flames began licking around the hem of his gown, Zozobra would begin to cry out over the PA system, giving vent to terrifying groans and screams as the flames rose higher and higher. His long arms would be made to writhe in agony and his amplified shrieks would rise above the cheers of the crowd. Then the flames would reach his belly and Old Man Gloom's cries would be drowned out by a welter of explosions and a spray of rockets and Roman candles. After that, everyone would be ready to party.

But in the village of La Ciénega that morning, no one was thinking about partying. There was too much to be done to prepare for their first foray into Santa Fe for several months. Father T.J. had offered them the use of his little church van, as they had hoped, so he and Tony had gathered up some tools and walked to the church to get the old Chevy ready to go.

Meanwhile, Lupe and Roberto resumed work on the Lieutenant's foot while he lay back, listening to the newscasts that had occupied his attention throughout a painful night.

"Two or three days and that foot will be as good as new," she said to Roberto.

"Still looks pretty bad to me," he said, "but I guess you know what you're doing."

"When we get back from town, I'll be able to make a poultice that will take care of that swelling," she said.

The Lieutenant took off the earphones.

"Do you and Tony pay much attention to the news, Mrs. Baca?"

"Tony does. He says the short wave is the only way he can get the truth."

"I used to listen back home in Tennessee. But the Army won't let you near a short wave radio these days. They say this stuff is seditious."

"Seditious?"

"You know, unpatriotic"

"Since when is the truth unpatriotic?"

"Hey, listen to that, Lieutenant. The truth she says," laughed Roberto.

The Lieutenant took a closer look at the woman who was doctoring his foot. There was little to mark her out from other Hispanic women of early middle age. Her black hair was cut short and her face still held much of the beauty that had adorned her youth. The overall impression was one of great strength, he decided. That plus a certain boldness that was different from the diffident Southern damsels he had known in Tennessee. He decided to confide in her.

"Mrs. Baca…"

"Call me Lupe. Please."

"All right, Lupe. Tell me. How much do you know about this fellow Emiliano?"

"Enough to know I don't like him one little bit."

"What do you think would happen up here if he was suddenly eliminated."

She looked at him sharply. "You mean killed?"

"Yes, killed."

"Is that what you're here for?" she laughed. "To eliminate our bad boy? Oh, that is so good! Emiliano will be there for sure strutting around like some kind of fancy rooster."

"I can't really discuss my orders."

"No, I guess not. But to answer your question, I think if he was eliminated like you say, there would be Hell to pay. There would be a struggle between two men to take his place. One is Alejandro, a man from Peñasco. One of his aunts is a neighbor of ours. He would not be so bad, but the other one–Peligro is his name–is a little mojado, a wet back, from way down there somewhere. If he took over, many people would die."

The Lieutenant let the subject drop. None of it made any sense. Why had they been ordered to eliminate Emiliano if someone even worse was waiting to take his place? More to the point, why didn't they just send a real force up here and clean these Fidelistas out once and for all? Was it because they no longer had confidence in their own troops' loyalty?

He put the earphones back on and resumed monitoring the radio. A man with a gruff, no nonsense voice was beginning a long monologue.

16

*P*ATRIOT RADIO IS ON THE AIR...

Hello out there, my fellow Americans. This is Colonel Dalton Lamar Beckwith of the Patriots, speaking to you from somewhere in the Rockies. As I look out over the great vistas of our beautiful West, I am reminded of just how courageous those pioneers were who first settled these lands. They braved blizzards, droughts, and attacks by hostile tribes, hauling their precious families and all their worldly possessions across a vast wilderness in search of a better life.

The weak perished, but the strong survived and their efforts made us a better nation, at least for a while. But what about us? Would we be up to those same challenges? After fifty years of indoctrination by left-wing teachers...after fifty years of the liberal propaganda dished up by writers, filmmakers, and newsmen, I wonder if we would make very good pioneers.

Imagine for a moment that a party of present day Americans is camped on the Mississippi trying to form a wagon train to California. These poor folks would have many issues to deal with before they ever started their journey. First they would have to choose a trail boss to guide them. They would have to decide whether the job should go to a woman or to a member of a minority for the sake of diversity. The best-qualified person might be passed over merely because of his race or gender.

Rules would then have to be drawn up concerning such things as the humane treatment of animals, antismoking policies, the prevention of sexual harassment, the free distributions of condoms and needles and regulations concerning work place safety. Persons who wished to carry firearms would have to have record checks. Since ownership of firearms is now so restricted, these latter day pioneers would have to be instructed in gun safety and marksmanship. Guidelines concerning nondiscrimination against persons with different life style choices would have to be laid down as well as policies governing assisted suicide and abortion. In addition, restrictions against hunting wild game or shooting at Native Americans would have to be developed along with rules restricting the practice of religion, especially the Christian religion.

By the time they finished creating all these rules and regulations, winter would very likely have set in, and our modern day pioneers would have had no choice except to return to their comfortable homes in the East and leave the pioneering to a tougher breed of men.

My friends, the worst part of this cautionary tale is that it is so close to the truth. For the past fifty years, we have blindly followed the lead of the Statists, letting them manipulate our beliefs and weaken our resolve, so that by now, we Americans are little more than a pathetic caricature of the real pioneers that once crossed this wilderness.

I ask you, my friends, what has become of our moral fiber, our sense of national purpose? They have been lost in the welter of demands for special privileges pressed on us by every minority group with the wit to claim victim status. Convenience and self-interest have replaced the time-honored values that made this country great, and our pride in America has been replaced by a fuzzy headed allegiance to some sort of world wide government.

Ignore your instincts, the Statists tell us. Forget your outmoded ideas of right and wrong and learn to live in a world where every wrong can be excused and every inequality can be corrected. Forget that you are an American. Bow down before the flag of the United Nations. Fall in line with our party line or we will brand you a bigot or a fanatic!

Over the years, we have gradually given into those threats, my friends, knowing in our hearts that we were headed toward a day when our national character would be utterly erased and America itself would be reduced to nothing but a gaggle of special interest groups.

That day is almost upon us. So let us stand together as Patriots and say, "I love my country, and I will defend it against anyone who seeks to weaken and divide it." My friends, we must remember that we are Americans first. What happens to our great experiment in democracy is more important than what happens to any one of us.

Thank God there are still a few men and women such as yourselves, men and women who love this country and want to save it from the grip of the Statists. If you are one of these true believers in the pioneer spirit that made this country great, then join us here in the still unconquered West.

17

"Esmeralda hasn't sounded this good for years," said Father T.J. patting the old van affectionately. "You are a good mechanic, my friend."

Tony turned off the ignition. He had adjusted the timing and cleaned the points, and the smooth sound of the engine was making him feel better too. It was good to have something to do to keep his mind off all the complications that were suddenly crowding into his life. As a finishing touch he topped off the gas tank with one of the five gallon cans that Father T.J. had been saving for an emergency, straining the fuel through a piece of cheesecloth to make sure no bits of dust made it into the tank.

"I could sweep her out," he asked hopefully. "Get rid of some of these spider webs."

"I'm sure Lupe would appreciate that," said Father T.J. "And while you're doing that I'll gather up some food. We ought to eat a bite before we go."

He hurried into the chapel and returned with a basket full of the tortillas from the Widow Flores. "We can't do much on an empty stomach," he said.

Tony laughed. "What a lady's man you are with the good cooks!"

Father T.J. did not rise to the bait because he was suddenly thinking about something far more important to him than food.

"Your wife is very courageous. Isn't she, Tony?"

"She don't back down for nobody, that's for sure."

"I have always admired her for that."

"Sometimes you just have to let her have her way."

"But she has been a good wife to you, I know."

"The best, Father. And a good cook too," he said, trying to bring the subject back around to safer territory.

"Myself, I am not courageous," said Father T.J.

"No one really knows how brave they are until they are tested, Father."

To Father T.J. it seemed that he had been tested all his life by a succession of bullies. In grade school he had been bookish and shy, the perfect foil for the swaggering toughs who regularly robbed him of his lunch money. In seminary he had become the target of a particularly bitter priest who teased him unmercifully about his inability to learn Greek. And finally, as a young priest in his first parish, he had been bullied by the head of the altar guild, a formidable matron who thought it her duty to control everything he did, his choice of music, his vestments and even his sermon topics. This was the point at which he had tried to fight back by growing his fierce looking beard, but it had fooled no one, least of all the matron, who kept after him relentlessly until he managed to beg a transfer to the little parish at La Ciénega. Here he had stayed, relieved to find no bullies waiting to torment him in that quiet village. He was happy for a few years, living the life that God had intended for his priests, and then the bullies had returned to torment him, terrible bullies in the form of Emiliano and his Fidelistas.

"God tests us all, my friend," he replied simply. "It is how we respond that makes the difference."

"Priests play by different rules, don't you think?"

"God expects the same of priests as He does of other men."

"He expects more sometimes," said Tony, thinking of a lonely bed without Lupe.

"True enough," said Father T.J., thinking much the same thing. Then focusing his attention on matters at hand, he said, "For one thing he expects us to be ready to administer his sacraments no matter where we go or what we do."

With that he hurried back to the chapel and retrieved the little leatherette kit that he carried when visiting the sick. It contained a small prayer book, a vial of holy water and a few sanctified wafers that looked like small, white poker chips.

"We just might be needing this," he said, slipping behind the wheel of the van.

As he drove the two of them back to where Lupe was waiting, Father T.J. occasionally slapped the end of his thick leather belt against his thigh as if spurring himself on to meet whatever unknown tests might lie ahead.

18

Two unmarked helicopters were being serviced behind a high security fence at Kirtland Air Force Base in Albuquerque. After the choppers were fueled and armed with rockets, the ground crews drove off, and a man in civilian clothes emerged from a nearby building with two young pilots, designated Taco One and Taco Two for that night's mission.

"Remember," he said, "if you don't hear from our man on the ground by 15:30 hours, you are to proceed with the attack. Target the stage and the escape routes. That's where the bad guys will be."

"That's where you think they'll be," corrected Taco One, who had already decided he didn't like this mission any better than he liked the man in the suit.

"We've made every effort to hold collateral damage to a minimum," said the suit, as if reciting a line he had learned by heart.

"We just call them dead civilians," said Taco Two.

"Look you two," said the suit curtly, "if you don't want to undergo a loyalty check, you'd better let this drop right now. I don't care whether you approve of this operation or not. This is not a debate. You have your orders, and you'd better carry them out!"

With that he turned on his heal and walked quickly away.

"I'd like to carry him out," said Taco One. "How the Hell does a jerk like that get put in charge of something like this?"

"Connections," said Taco Two. "Big time, Statist connections. This mess must have been planned by folks way on up the food chain."

"Which means we get busted good if we screw up."

"We could wind up in Minot chasing cigarette smugglers."

"Ah yes, the frozen north. This mission is looking better all the time. Let's have another look at those maps."

The city of Albuquerque was sandwiched between the Rio Grande River on one side and Sandia Mountain on the other. This huge escarpment rose to an elevation of over eleven thousand feet, nearly six thousand feet above the level of the river and walled off the eastern side of the city. Sixty miles to the northeast lay the city of Santa Fe, spilled out across the southernmost foothills of the Sangre de Cristos like a set of adobe colored building blocks. The pilots planned to follow Highway 14, the old Turquoise Trail, past Madrid and Gallisteo and arrive at their firing point just as Zozobra was set on fire. They knew that in that moment of celebration no one would pay the slightest attention to the muffled sound of their rotors, and that death would rain down upon the crowd without warning. It would be a slaughter.

19

Lupe was waiting impatiently when the men got back to the house with Esmeralda.

"Where have you two been?" she said. "Joy riding?" She climbed up into the van with two neatly folded grocery sacks under her arm and sat herself down behind the driver's seat.

"I brought some tortillas," said Father T.J. offering her the basket as an explanation. "Maybe we should eat before we go."

"We don't have time for food right now," said Lupe. "We need to get in there and get out before they all get too drunk."

"Lots of them stay drunk all the time," said Tony, climbing in after her.

"Those we can handle," said Lupe. "It's the new drunks I worry about."

Father T.J. relinquished the Widow Flores' tortillas to Roberto, and without another word, headed the van toward Santa Fe.

Obedient to his grandmother's superstition, Roberto made sure not to watch the little van out of sight. Instead, he carried the basket of fresh tortillas to the Lieutenant, who was still lying on the couch with his foot resting on a stack of pillows.

"You want something to chew on, sir?"

"Let's see if we can contact Kirtland first."

Roberto retrieved their little radio from the shed, but when the Lieutenant switched it on, nothing happened. No lights. No beeps. No buzzes. He shook it vigorously. He held it upside down and tapped it. Finally, he slapped it hard with the palm of his hand. Nothing.

"Damn it!" he said. "You'd think they'd at least give us a working radio."

"Remember, this is the U.S. Army we're talking about," said Roberto.

"We might still be able to make it to our firing point with the help of that van of theirs."

"If we got caught, they'd come straight down here and shoot Father T.J. Probably Tony and Lupe too."

"Would you rather leave the job to the helicopters?"

"Sir, without this radio there's no way we can stop them anyway."

The Lieutenant pried off the back.

"Just look at this!" he said. "One of these gizmos is completely missing."

The cleanly severed wires told the Lieutenant that his worst fears might be coming true. He knew there were deepening divisions within the army. Some units were said to be "loyal," which meant that they sympathized with the Statists, and supported the current President. Other units were said to sympathize with the anti-government militia movement. So far, discipline had been maintained, but the tensions were growing, and Lieutenant McDowell felt certain that their sabotaged radio might be a sign that those tensions had reached a breaking point. Precisely which faction might profit from a blood bath at the Santa Fe Fiesta he had not yet worked out.

"So why send us up here in the first place?" said Roberto.

"Someone wanted to be doubly sure they got Emiliano?"

"More likely the right hand doesn't know what the left hand is doing," said McDowell. "Our orders came from division headquarters, but some one higher up, who doesn't give a damn about us or whether we ever get back to Kirtland, wants that rocket attack to proceed at all costs."

"So we're up here risking our lives for nothing."

"Looks like it."

"I'd like to get my hands on the brass hats who left us hanging out here to dry," said Roberto. "With no radio we can't even arrange a rendezvous."

"One thing at a time, Corporal. We still have our orders."

"Whoever planned this mess doesn't care about extracting us or cutting down casualties at Fiesta."

"Looks like it, all right."

"So what do we do?"

"I took an oath to uphold the Constitution, Corporal. And so far that means obeying orders."

"The Constitution doesn't say anything about rocket attacks on civilians, sir. Whoever dreamed this up doesn't give a rat's ass about your precious Constitution."

"You got that right," said the Lieutenant. "In fact, you just might be closer to the real truth about all this than we realize."

20

Fr. T.J. took the long way around to drive into Santa Fe. He used the road that looped behind the old racetrack to reach Rodeo Road, and from there he drove to Old Pecos Trail and followed that down to the Plaza area. There was less chance of encountering land mines that way. Less chance too of encountering people, since the southern half of the city was now virtually deserted.

With the state capital relocated to Albuquerque and the tourist industry dead, Santa Fe had shrunk to less than a quarter of the size it had reached when the immigration of disaster wary Californians was at its height. Whole neighborhoods were becoming dilapidated as the remaining citizens "borrowed" freely from the derelict homes of former residents. A gate here, a few adobes there, even some shrubs and shade trees had been dug up and carted off. During the coming winter these same houses would provide a ready supply of firewood just for the taking, and the process of dilapidation would continue.

At least that would take some pressure off the search for mature piñon trees to harvest for firewood. Piñons had been the fuel of choice in Santa Fe, since the days when men would go into the hills and return before dark with their little burros loaded down with faggots of the hot burning wood. In the early days they would congregate in Burro Alley near the Plaza to peddle their wares, but now that all the nearby trees had been cut, the modern day woodcutters were doing good to find enough piñon for themselves and a few friends. Gathering enough wood to last out the winter had become every man's obsession, especially now that fall was coming on.

Winter in Santa Fe was cold, but it was never really harsh. At night the temperature might dip below zero, making a good crackling fire more than just a luxury. Then the next morning when the almighty sun had risen a few degrees above the horizon, the chill would have disappeared and even the coldest day would seem almost pleasant.

The Spanish colonists had chosen the site for their capitol with great care. If they had settled a hundred miles to the east they would have been exposed to the freezing blizzards that swept down the eastern slopes of the mountains, and if they had chosen a lower altitude, they would have suffered from heat and drought. But here in Santa Fe, at an altitude of seven thousand feet, in the foothills of the western slopes of the Sangre de Cristos, they found cool summers, tolerable winters, and in their day at least, a good supply of both wood and water.

In this perfect spot, the Spanish had built one of the most isolated outposts of their empire. For nearly two hundred and fifty years they had prospered with little interference from the outside world. Then came the Mexican War and, the victorious Americans took over, bringing with them their army and their Santa Fe Trail. The town quickly filled with blue coats, teamsters and adventurers of every kind. Then the railroad was completed, and a new population of consumptives, artists, and dreamers joined the mix. Soon Santa Fe began to take on the unique character that had marked it throughout the twentieth century when it cast itself first as a health resort, then as an artists' colony, and finally as a hideaway for the rich and famous.

With the coming of the Fidelistas, the City Different had reverted to type and once again became what it should always have remained, a small Spanish village, very isolated and a bit rundown around the edges.

Tony and Lupe took a certain pride in their old hometown, and they were slightly annoyed by its disreputable appearance.

"Just look at this place," said Lupe. "It's getting to be such a mess!"

"These empty houses give me the creeps," said Tony. "Blocks and blocks of them, all deserted. No smoke from the chimneys. No cars in the driveways. No nothing."

"I hope you know where we're going," said Father T.J.

"Just head toward the Plaza," said Lupe.

It took a few tries but she finally located the right shop a few blocks from the Plaza. They parked the van around the corner and walked the rest of the way so as not to advertise their presence.

The door was easily broken in. There were no lights inside, but they could see that the shop itself had been stripped to the walls. Fortunately, they found everything they needed in a small storeroom behind the counter. There were shelves loaded with of all kinds of dried plants: bins of leaves, bundles of twigs and roots and big apothecary jars filled with seedpods. The air was thick with the odor of desert vegetation. Lupe quickly began loading her sacks with treasures from this trove of medicinal plants. Every move she made raised a small cloud of dust, but she continued her search identifying the plants with the help of Fr. T.J's flashlight.

"There's a lot here we could use," she said. "I just wish I had brought more sacks."

"We can always come back later," said Tony, fibbing a bit to hurry her along.

"Here's some empty boxes," she said. "You two come in here and help me fill them up with some of this stuff from up on the shelves where I can't reach."

Tony and Father T.J. did as she asked, and so by the merest chance, they were safely out of sight when the front door burst open and the screaming started.

21

Peligro started searching for the perfect girl for Emiliano as soon as he arrived in Santa Fe that afternoon. There were plenty of teenagers to choose from. The young people had come out in force to enjoy Fiesta. Unlike their elders, they were not particularly afraid of the Fidelistas, believing, like teenagers everywhere, that they were personally indestructible. Boredom drove them from the safety of their homes, and they gathered in the Plaza, dressed in their best and ready for some excitement.

After one sweep of the crowd, Peligro settled on his victim, a pretty, young girl sitting with a group of her friends on a park bench near the bandstand in the Plaza. She had long dark hair, a thin, aristocratic face and the body of a grown woman, without any hint of the plumpness of a Tina Roybal. According to the ages of her friends, she was about fourteen, but she looked more like twenty, and Peligro was sure that Emiliano would like her very much.

The rest was easy.

First he flushed her out by walking slowly towards her, staring directly at her all the while. Once she felt his fierce eyes upon her, she became flustered. She stood up and tried to move away from him, foolishly leaving her friends. Peligro followed her quietly, keeping a discreet distance, but shepherding her always toward less crowded areas of the Plaza. Her panic grew as he kept up his dogged chase. She began walking faster and faster, until without knowing quite how it had happened, she found herself alone on a deserted street with only her relentless pursuer standing between her and the safety of the Fiesta crowds.

She ran then, making a headlong dash for safety, but he cut her off, grabbed her up like a sack of fresh chilies and brutally shoved her through the doorway of the old herbalist's shop. Once inside he grabbed her by the wrists and spun her around with her back to the wall. That was when she screamed like the frightened child that she was.

"It is useless, señorita," smiled Peligro. "There is no one to help you. But do not worry, I will not harm you. I have been ordered only to bring you to Emiliano. That is all."

The girl screamed again, so Peligro slapped her carefully a time or two, being mindful of the bruises.

Tony, Lupe, and Father T.J. peeked out of the storeroom where they had been working to see what was going on, but Peligro was much too intent on his victim to notice them. The slaps had inspired him.

"You are very pretty, señorita," he said. "That is why I chose you."

The girl shook her head as if to wake herself from a bad dream that would not go away.

"I chose you for a very important mission." continued Peligro. "Our great leader has decided to take you with him to the town of Creed, in Colorado. There he will give you to another very important leader of men. Your beauty is a prize for such men, señorita, like gold or diamonds for kings."

Father T.J. was aghast.

"Do you see who that is?" he whispered.

They could all see clearly that the girl struggling in Peligro's grasp was their little neighbor, Paquita, the sister of Ricardo and Joselito.

Tony motioned his friend to be quiet, restraining him with a firm hand. He could see the pistol at Peligro's belt, and he knew that any attempt to interfere would be fatal for all of them.

The little Nicaraguan had begun unbuttoning the girl's white shirt.

"Since you are such an important gift, I will have to make sure you don't have some ugly birth mark or scar to spoil your beauty. Our leader wants you to be perfect."

Peligro produced the short piece of rope he had brought with him for this purpose and tied the girl's wrists. Then he looped the other end of the rope over a hook on the wall and pulled it taut so that her arms were arched back over her head and she could not get away.

He finished unbuttoning her shirt and pulled the tail out of the waistband of her jeans so that it hung loose around her hips. Then he began to work on the demure undergarment she wore beneath her shirt. He did not bother with the little hooks, but took a large knife from his belt and simply cut the brassiere away, leaving Paquita's beautiful breasts completely exposed. She fought against the rope, trying to avoid his touch. Peligro admired her heaving breasts for a moment and then he reached out to touch them gently, almost reverently. In the dim light they stood out clearly, cupped in his swarthy hands like two frightened white rabbits with very pink noses.

"We have to stop this," whispered Father T.J., straining against Tony's grip.

"He has a pistol to go with that knife, Father. We wouldn't have a chance."

"But..."

"Quiet or you'll get us killed. Lupe too."

He could feel Lupe's grip tighten on his shoulder and he knew that she was fighting back the urge to cry out. She had witnessed the whole attack, but she too had seen the pistol.

Meanwhile, Peligro continued to fondle Paquita's breasts for what seemed like a very long time, then he moved his hands down her body and slowly but carefully caressed her buttocks through the fabric of her jeans. Then he pulled her to him and held her tight against his body while he began thrusting against her in a slow, but unmistakable rhythm. He kept this up despite her pitiful moans until Father T.J. had to look away. The more she struggled the closer he pulled her to his crotch until finally he reached a shuddering climax and let her fall back from his grip.

"That was very nice," he said approvingly. "Sometimes it is nice for girls to struggle, especially when a man is wearing silk underwear. Do you wear silk underwear, señorita? I would like to see for myself, but I promised Emiliano that I would not touch you. And I have not touched you, have I?"

The dark little man laughed sardonically and took one last admiring look at her naked breasts. Then he was all business.

"Now, I will untie your hands and let you fix your clothing," he said. "Then we will go back and watch the burning of this monster of yours. You will have a front row seat because you will be with Emiliano himself."

When she was ready, he retied her hands behind her back and looped the other end of the rope around his wrist. "Stay with me, señorita and you will not be hurt. Try to run away and you will see how fast this rope can pull you down."

He dragged her out the door, and the two of them headed for the Plaza. Only then did Father T.J. let out a long held breath.

"Madre de Dios! What are we going to do?" he said. "We must do something to help that girl."

Lupe's face seemed frozen in a fierce scowl. She had borne the sight of Peligro taking his pleasure with her little neighbor in silence. But now she found a terrible anger growing in her heart, and it took her a moment to find ordinary words for a reply.

"We are going to go and get her back, that's what," she said, as if answering the most obvious of questions. "We are going to teach that pig a lesson too."

"But not tonight," said Tony.

"No, not tonight," agreed Lupe. "First we make preparations. We know where they are going. There is only one road. There is a good chance we can stop them before they get to Creed."

She returned to the storeroom for a moment and came back with her arms loaded with sacks. "Help me carry those boxes," she said. "If we take good care of our new Lieutenant maybe he and Roberto will help us rescue that poor girl."

22

Santa Fe's spacious Plaza had been the very heart of the city since it was founded in 1608. In those early days, the big quadrangle of adobe dwellings had doubled as a crude fortification. Here the people gathered for protection against roving bands of Commanches and other tribes that sometimes visited death and destruction on colonists and Pueblo People alike.

The north side of the Plaza was dominated by a huge, one-story building, known as the Palace of the Governors. This formidable structure, the seat of government during colonial times, had walls nearly three feet thick, sheltering dozens of offices and apartments that opened onto a shady courtyard with a well of sweet water that was still good to drink. The Palace of the Governors had undergone many face-lifts over the years according to the whims of various viceroys and governors. It had served as a residence, a courthouse, and as a suite of offices for state employees. Its final incarnation had been as the New Mexico Museum of History, and as such it was now shuttered and locked, awaiting the return of the tourists.

The south portal of this building faced the dusty square and made a cozy place to sit on sunny winter days. For centuries the Pueblo people had spread their blankets there, selling their crafts, first to the Spanish and later to the Anglos.

But on this first night of Fiesta there were no Pueblo People there at all. With the coming of the Fidelistas, the Pueblo People had withdrawn to their ancestral lands, refusing to have anything to do with the ugly little conflict that threatened to engulf them. Only the Spanish remained to celebrate their Fiesta. They did their best to fill the Plaza with as much excitement as might have been generated in happier times by much larger crowds when both tourists and Pueblo People had joined the party.

Food stalls sweetened the air with wonderful odors: rounds of fry bread cooking in vats of hot grease, crispy chicharones sizzling in cast iron skillets, and green chili stew bubbling in huge caldrons. Best of all were the fresh sopaipillas, bobbing like little pillows next to the fry bread before being scooped up, covered with honey, and greedily devoured by hungry children.

It was good to hear their happy voices sounding across the Plaza, blending with the music from a dozen boom boxes that created a rhythmic traffic jam in the background. Lonely people starved for the chance to talk gathered in little groups and swapped rumors about the fighting or gossiped about the eternal questions of love, sex, illness and death. For their part, the teenagers were too restless to sit and talk for long, and they strolled about showing off for each other and flirting shamelessly.

This was Fiesta as it had always been, and even the presence of the advance party of Fidelistas had not dampened the crowd's pleasure at finding their ancient celebration still essentially intact. Then shortly before dusk, the main force of Fidelistas had arrived. Several trucks parked near the Plaza and dozens of men including Emiliano himself piled out.

The mood of the crowd had changed at once. People lowered their voices, speaking in conspiratorial whispers and eyeing the pistols the guerillas wore at their belts. The shouts of the children had died away as mothers gathered their broods together, and even the delicious odors from the food stalls disappeared beneath the stench of the trucks' exhaust.

Its good mood broken, the crowd had begun to desert the Plaza and gravitate toward Ft. Marcy Park, where Zozobra awaited his doom. Vendors moved among them, selling jars of homemade beer or bottles of hard apple cider to people who were already shambling along in a tipsy sort of way. The most serious drinkers had brought their own supply of moonshine, enough to maintain their holiday mood throughout the entire three days of Fiesta and beyond.

But not everyone was full of holiday spirit, for among the crowd trudging up Bishop's Lodge Road in the deepening gloom, was Joselito Vigil, who was searching for his sister. It was not like her to simply disappear, and he was sure that something had gone terribly wrong. At last he saw a familiar face he could turn to for help. It was Mr. Zamora, his old grade school crossing guard, who was tagging along at the rear of the crowd.

"Mr. Zamora," the boy called out.

"¿Quien es?" said the old man, peering at the boy in the gloom.

"It's me, Mr. Zamora. Joselito Vigil."

Mr. Zamora did not have the slightest idea who this slim young man was, but he replied as he always did in these situations.

"My, but you have grown so tall, Joselito!"

"Mr. Zamora, my sister has disappeared!"

"How old is your sister?"

"Fourteen."

"Sometimes fourteen year old girls like to disappear for a while, amigo."

"Not Paquita. She is really missing, Mr. Zamora. I can't find her anywhere."

"All right. I will help you search. Tell me what she is wearing."

Joselito tried his best to describe Paquita. Then he said, "Do you have your whistle?"

The old man produced his old, brass police whistle, which he carried with him as a badge of his former office.

"Please blow that thing if you see her," said the boy. "I will come right away."

Then he hurried off, more certain than ever that his sister was in some kind of trouble, and that it was his fault for not looking after her on the first night of Fiesta.

23

Some families with elderly members who could not manage the long walk from the Plaza were already waiting for the show to begin at Ft. Marcy Park. They had spread their blankets in the best spots nearest the stage, and now prepared to defend their turf against the new arrivals from the Plaza. Competition for the few remaining front row spots was fierce, and the festive mood was almost broken as a few shoving matches broke out.

The Fidelistas stood about doing nothing to help. Even though they had chased off most of the law officers in the region, they did not seem to feel that it was their responsibility to help restore order now. The amount of beer and cider that had been consumed by the crowd did not help, and the situation almost got out of hand before some quick-witted stagehand fired up the big Diesel generator and powered up the lights and the music.

The crowd settled down quickly, and before long the honor guard in the costume of Spanish soldiers trooped onto the stage leading the Fiesta queen and her beautiful princesses. A tall man sporting a plumed helmet and a full black beard stepped to the microphone. In perfect Spanish he read aloud the proclamation by Captain General DeVargas establishing the Fiesta in 1711, as a celebration of the reconquest of Santa Fe after the Pueblo Revolt.

The audience listened in silence, reflecting on the fact that this could well be the last reading of the proclamation for a long time. Everyone knew that the struggle with the Fidelistas could put an end to the celebration of their precious Fiesta forever.

Following the reading, the crowd's mood revived as troops of costumed children came on to the stage and performed a series of folk dances. Then, when a traditional mariachi band began to play, the crowd really began whooping it up in anticipation of the event they had all come to see.

Traditionally, Zozobra was set on fire by a fanciful figure known as the "fire dancer." This role was played by a young man in a red and orange body suit who would dance around the huge effigy, brandishing a flaming torch while the monster muttered and groaned and rolled his fearsome eyes in comic terror of the flames to come.

The fire dancer was usually greeted with a loud cheer from the crowd and an even louder groan from Old Man Gloom, but this time his dance of death was interrupted by Emiliano himself, who climbed onto the stage and strode toward the microphone. Some of his men fired their pistols into the air to silence the ripple of protest that sprang up from the crowd when the music stopped and the dancer ceased his gyrations. At the sound of the shots the 'fire dancer' scuttled out of sight, leaving Emiliano alone at center stage with Zozobra looming over his shoulder like some kind of sinister henchman.

The great leader stood there for a moment, enjoying the frightened looks on the faces of many in the hushed crowd. Then he began pacing back and forth with his arms folded across his chest, in unconscious imitation of a certain Italian Fascist of the mid twentieth century. He stopped his pacing occasionally and looked at the crowd. First he glared at them fiercely. Then he assumed a statesmanlike pose looking serenely out over their heads. And finally he cast his smile upon them like a blessing.

He picked up the microphone and tried to speak, but no sound came from the PA system. He fiddled with the various switches and wires but there was still no sound. Desperately he began pounding the microphone against his palm, and suddenly the sound system came to life.

"Madre de Dios," he muttered, his words suddenly blaring out over the crowd as if Old Man Gloom was suddenly calling on the Blessed Virgin. Some drunks and a few children laughed, but Emiliano raised a hand to silence them. It would not do to have these people laughing at their leader.

"Silence!" he shouted, and again it seemed that Zozobra was speaking. This time no one laughed.

"People of Santa Fe," he said, beginning with his benevolent look. "I bring you good news. We have destroyed another convoy from Albuquerque. Soon the Yankees will no longer dare to enter our lands, and we will be victorious."

At this point Peligro arrived, dragging the girl after him. He brought her out on stage to stand beside the great leader, and for a long moment Emiliano forgot about his speech and about the crowd and simply looked at the girl.

She was truly beautiful despite her tear-stained cheeks and downcast eyes. There was nothing like the really young ones, he thought, and this one was special. He took the rope that still bound the girl's hands and pulled her toward him. She resisted, but in the end she had no choice but to stand next to him while he resumed his rambling speech.

He harangued the crowd about the seizure of Spanish lands by the Yankee imperialists. He told them about the prosperity that they would enjoy when the Southwest was reunited with the People's Republic of Mexico. And he reminded them that the Fidelistas were now in complete control of their destiny.

All the while he was tugging Paquita closer to him, draping one arm over her shoulder so that his hand was brought closer and closer to those beautiful breasts that had so inspired Peligro. Her struggles only served to brush their incredible softness past his fingertips, and this seductive friction seemed to lift Emiliano to new rhetorical heights. His words came tumbling out, making even less sense, but no one in the crowd noticed because they were spell bound by the sight of his left hand reaching down inside her shirt and exploring the wonders to be found there.

Everyone in the crowd was riveted by the sight of this beautiful young girl, one of their own children, being publicly ravished by a man who was so confidant of his power that he could do whatever he pleased, no matter how shameful, without fear of reprisal.

Emiliano now moved his explorations below her waist. He began to caress her hips and buttocks, and this brought him to such a peak of excitement that he found it difficult to speak at all, and he fell silent while he tried to gather his wits.

As it happened, this moment of silence allowed Peligro's keen ears to pick up the unmistakable sound of helicopters approaching from the south. Instantly he guessed what was about to happen. Without hesitating, he grabbed Emiliano and the girl, shoving them away from the microphone toward the rear of stage, where he pushed them down behind a pile of adobes. Emiliano protested loudly, unable to fathom what madness had suddenly possessed his trusted lieutenant. But Peligro paid no heed to his protests and as the helicopters drew closer, he threw himself on top of both Emiliano and the girl and waited for what was sure to come.

24

The two unmarked helicopters had taken off from Kirtland Air Force Base and flown around the northern flank of Sandia Mountain. Once beyond that barrier, they made for the Turquoise Trail, which connected the three little mining towns of Golden, Madrid, and Cerrillos. There they dropped back down to the deck and followed the old highway at treetop level, pretending to evade radar that they knew did not exist. It was easier to think of the mission as a training exercise rather than to deal with the fact that they were about to attack a crowd of defenseless civilians.

They snaked along the winding road in single file, leaving a spray of sand and some very startled jack rabbits in their wake, passing through the town of Madrid with the ruins of its coal tipple rising above them on the right. At the outskirts of Santa Fe they picked up Old Pecos Trail and followed it all the way to the Plaza, blasting over the big obelisk at its center like a pair of angry whirlwinds before stopping to hover over the huge, pink edifice of the Scottish Rite Temple. This was to be their firing point, where they had expected to see the flames from Old Man Gloom, but there was nothing except darkness in front of them.

"Taco Two to Taco One."

"Taco One, no joy on the bon fire."

"Affirmative, Taco Two."

"So, what gives?"

"Don't know. Don't care. You know the drill. If we haven't heard from our guys on the ground by now then it's up to us."

"Roger that. Is your radio working?"

"Five by five."

"Mine too, and I'm hearing nada, zip, nothing from down there."

"All right then. It's definitely the shits, but you heard what the suit told us. 'Launch rockets and get the Hell back to Kirtland.'"

And that is precisely what they did.

25

The first rocket came with a loud whoosh! Like some kind of cosmic prank, it landed squarely in the center of Old Man Gloom, blasting him into instant conflagration and sending bushels of firecrackers and Roman candles raining down on the crowd. As these begin to explode, the other rockets followed in quick succession. Most of them went over the stage and landed in the parking lot beyond, but a few fell short and did more damage to the people of Santa Fe than all the Commanche raiding parties ever thought about doing.

Untidy body parts gyrated through the air and landed in bizarre attitudes all over the area. As the noise of the explosions died away, the inarticulate screams and groans of the wounded rose like a fog over the scene. There was no sound at all from the departing helicopters.

The force of the blasts dazed Emiliano. Although he was himself a master maker of bombs, he had always made sure that he was nowhere near the spot where they actually exploded. The crushing impact and deafening noise of the attack came as a profound shock to him. Instinctively he reached out for the girl, who was screaming hysterically. Her plans for a happy evening with her friends had somehow turned into the most hideous kind of nightmare from which there seemed no escape, and Emiliano's mindless embrace did nothing to comfort her.

Peligro was the first to recover his senses. He stood up and looked around. One of the unexploded firecrackers lay next to Emiliano and the girl. He kicked it to the side where it sputtered out weakly. Something large and bloody lay on top of the pile of adobes that had protected them, but he ignored it and helped Emiliano and the girl to their feet. He led them toward the trucks where the men would be gathering to await orders. Now was the time for the men to see for themselves that their leader had escaped unharmed.

26

Meanwhile, in Washington D.C., a cabinet meeting had just adjourned. The President had been forceful and unyielding. Some doubts had been expressed over the wisdom of the plan and a few had questioned whether the situation was really serious enough to call for such a precedent setting step. But their objections were quieted when the members of the cabinet were reminded that the former President himself would be flying in to speak to the nation. This calmed their fears considerably because they all remembered how the old man could seduce the voters into believing just about anything he wanted them to believe. In the end the President's plan was approved unanimously.

The truth was that there was never any doubt about the eventual outcome of the vote. Now well into its second term, the Administration functioned like a well-oiled steamroller. Whatever the President wanted, and that was sometimes quite a lot, the President got. Some nitpickers complained about the legalities, but that was seen as nothing more than face-saving rhetoric. In the end they cast their votes the way the President wanted and departed with orders to instruct their departments to obey the Administrations orders without question.

Cho Lin Wok, the young man generally conceded to be the President's most brilliant adviser, had sat quietly through the entire meeting. He was hoping to learn a thing or two about how the President dominated people in situations such as this. It was an ability the President had in abundance and one which Cho Lin Wok greatly admired.

Now, however, he was hurrying to try a little dominating of his own. He needed to put a stop to a conversation between a certain senator, one of the President's last remaining opponents, and the notably spineless secretary of education. Even from a distance, it was easy to see the conspiratorial nature of the little whispering session. Furtive looks and attitudes of shock and disbelief left little doubt about what was passing between the two. It was the sort of thing that needed to be nipped in the bud, and Wok knew that the President would approve of even the strongest measures to put a stop to such disloyalty.

"Oh, Senator," called Cho Lin.

The senator looked up like the proverbial deer in headlights and backed quickly away from the suddenly ashen secretary of education.

"Yes?"

"Is anything wrong? You look worried."

"Worried? Why, no. I don't know what you're talking about."

"These are dangerous times we live in, Senator. I don't blame you for being worried."

"Don't talk nonsense, young man."

"Perhaps you would feel better if you had some protection."

"I don't need any protection!"

"Oh, but I insist." Cho Lin signaled to a Secret Service agent who was stationed just down the hall. "Agent Sommers here will look after you," he said.

"But I…"

"Agent Sommers," said Cho Lin imperiously, "I want you to make sure the senator here gets home safely. And then I want you to make sure he stays there."

"Yes, sir."

"But this is outrageous," sputtered the senator.

"It's for your own protection," smiled Cho Lin. "We don't want you getting kidnapped by any of these radical groups."

"I know what you're up to Wok!" said the senator, "and you won't get away with it."

"Maybe not, Senator, but for now, you are going home and staying there."

He gave a nod and perhaps the tiniest bit of a wink to Agent Sommers, who led the senator away, while Cho Lin turned to focus his gaze on the secretary of education.

"That was very unwise, Mr. Secretary," he said. "What if someone leaks word to the press about the President's decision? The suspicion would fall on you. For your sake I hope there are no leaks. None at all."

Just then there was the sound of high heels clipping rapidly toward them down the marble hallway. It was one of the President's secretaries.

"Mr. Wok," she called out. "The President wants to talk to you before you leave. In the Oval Office, sir."

"Right!" said Cho Lin Wok, releasing the secretary of education from his gaze. "Just tidying up a few loose ends here. Please tell the President that I'll be right with her."

SATURDAY
SEPTEMBER ELEVENTH

27

That night the first snow of the season fell on Santa Fe. It was only a light dusting, but it served to whiten the famous horse's head, which had been etched high on the mountainside by an ancient forest fire. Except for this distinguishing mark Santa Fe's mountain was rather ordinary. It was only about twelve thousand feet tall with a rather uninspiring crest. It did a workman like job of generating rain in the summer and snow in the winter, but the people of Santa Fe loved it mainly because it was theirs. Some felt the pride of ownership so strongly that they had chosen to remain close to their mountain even after the Fidelistas arrived.

First light glimmered on the summit and began caressing the fresh fields of snow like a lover's kiss. Dawn in Santa Fe was always crisp and clean, without the outrageous colors of the sunset. In a few weeks the aspens would begin to add gold to the color scheme. The beautiful display would begin as a thin band of color near timberline, broadening each day until the slopes were almost completely yellow.

But today there was only the snow frosted pines and firs for the sun to work on. The morning light worked its way slowly down the mountain until it reached Santa Fe itself, where it quickly melted the little snow that had fallen there and infused the flowers that still blossomed in a hundred courtyards with brilliant color.

Finally the sun's rays reached the tiny window above Father T.J's bed and splashed the opposite wall with a brilliant swatch of light that awakened him from a hard won sleep.

The chill of the first snowfall had invaded his little room and he hopped out of bed to scrabble together a small fire in the beehive fireplace near his cot. This familiar little chore reminded him that it was already past time to gather firewood for the elderly residents of his village. After the propane deliveries stopped, La Ciénega had to depend entirely on wood stoves and fireplaces for all of its cooking and heating. Father T.J. had organized crews of teenagers to help gather wood for those who could not do it for themselves. In these mountains, it was essential for every home to have plenty of firewood stacked beside its back door.

Father T.J. enjoyed getting out in the fresh air and working off a few pounds in a good cause. He would begin each expedition by commandeering two or three pickup trucks along with enough kids to fill them with firewood in a single afternoon. Then they would drive far out along the rutted BLM roads and find dead piñon trees to cut. The boys would set to work with axes and chain saws, and the girls would stack the wood in the trucks. They would continue working in this way until just before sunset when they would build a big campfire and enjoy the feast that the women of the village always provided. For Father T.J. it was one of the best parts of the fall season.

"Father T.J. it's me, Ricardo! Wake up!"

An insistent pounding at his door interrupted Father T.J.'s reverie about crackling campfires and the Widow Quintana's enchiladas. Quickly he put on his clothes and stumbled to the door where he found the boy standing on the step with tears streaming down his face.

Without a word, Father T.J. swept him up into a full strength abrazo, a sort of Latino bear hug, that told the boy he had found a strong right arm to lean on.

"Oh, padrecito," he said, sobbing into the priest's shoulder. "They have taken Paquita, and Joselito has disappeared."

"Tell me about it," said Father T.J.

"Last night we rode Rayito into Santa Fe to see Zozobra."

"Yes?"

"All three of us."

"Poor Rayito."

"Joselito and I walked most of the way," said the boy proudly.

"Good for you," said the priest.

"It all happened so fast, Father. First Paquita was there talking with her friends and then she was gone and Joselito went to look for her. Then we saw her again up on the stage with that man, Emiliano, and he was touching her in bad places and I was ashamed!"

The poor girl, thought the priest. First that devil, Peligro, then Emiliano. Surely God would punish these men who did such things to a child.

"He was touching her all over, Father. Under her shirt and other places you are not supposed to touch people and everyone was watching."

The boy began to sob, while the priest hugged him all the tighter and considered their situation.

The night before, the priest had stayed late at the Baca's home while they planned how they would rescue Paquita. At midnight they had tuned in to the regular Fidelista broadcast from Truchas. Most nights there was nothing but crude propaganda along with some coded messages for their units all across the Southwest. But last night they had heard the voice of Emiliano himself, nearly hysterical with rage.

"Tonight we were attacked for the first time by helicopters," he said. "Many innocent people were wounded, and some were killed, but I, at least, am safe, so everything is under control. Tomorrow I leave for an important meeting in Colorado. Be warned that if anyone makes trouble while I am gone, they will pay a heavy price."

Thanks to Emiliano's foolhardy announcement of his own travel plans, they had one piece of the puzzle in hand. All that remained had been to decide where to intercept him. But now this child was bringing him fresh intelligence. If the girl had been on stage she might very well have been wounded. No mention of her by Emiliano. And what part would Joselito play in all this now that he was missing too?

"What happened next, Ricardo?" asked the priest gently.

"I don't know exactly, Father. There were all these explosions and I got knocked down, and when I got up a lot of people were dead. Old Mr. Zamora, the crossing guard, was dead. He was all blown open." The boy made a face.

"And what about Paquita and Joselito?"

"I climbed up on stage to look for her, and I saw some Fidelistas pushing her into a big truck. And then they just drove off."

"She did not appear to be hurt?"

"No."

"And Joselito?"

"I told you, Father. I never saw him again. He might have gotten blown open like Mr. Zamora or he might have tried to follow Paquita. Me and Rayito waited for him a long time, but he never came back."

Father T.J. looked the boy in the eye. "Now listen," he said. "I am leaving this morning to go and look for your brother and your sister. While I am gone you must take care of your mother."

"But the Fidelistas have Paquita. There is nothing you can do."

"Haven't I told you that with God, all things are possible?"

"Yes."

"Well, I believe He has already provided us with the help we will need," said the priest enigmatically. "Now go and see about your mother."

"I left Rayito saddled all night too," the boy confessed.

"Well, take care of Rayito first, but don't forget your mother."

"She cried all night."

"When I get back and everyone is safe, we will give thanks to God."

Father T.J. watched the boy hurry away. Only yesterday the two brothers had peddled happily up that same road with nothing more important than a soccer ball on their minds. Now everything had become deadly serious and there was no telling what other surprises the next few hours would bring.

28

Lupe was also up with the dawn. She had been lying awake, thinking of her vengeance against Peligro. They were not pretty thoughts. Not pretty at all. For some women vengeance, or "la venganza" as the Spanish call it, is an eye-gouging, groin kicking sort of thing. Such women are not to be crossed, and Lupe was feeling very crossed indeed. She had taken the vile attack on Paquita as a direct attack upon herself. It had been a sexual assault of the worst sort: brutish, crude, and meant to humiliate. With the images of that attack burning in her mind, Lupe had experienced a curious sort of transformation that empowered her to do unspeakable things. Better for Emiliano and Peligro that an entire platoon from Special Forces had been after them than a vengeful Lupe Baca.

Like Father T.J., she hurried to get fires going in the living room fireplace and in the kitchen stove. There she started making the coffee and cooking breakfast for four. This morning she had decided to make Tony's favorite: huevos rancheros with plenty of refried beans, Spanish rice, chorizo and flour tortillas to sop it all up with.

Soon the smell of the coffee and the sound of the chorizo frying in the pan awakened the men, but even the promise of a good breakfast could not draw them from their beds until the chill was off the room. They had been up late studying the maps.

While the men were talking strategy, Lupe had prepared a foot soak for the Lieutenant. Following the directions in her grandmother's journal, she had chosen the roots of one plant and the leaves of another, boiling them down until they formed a cloudy, foul smelling soup. As a final touch she added a teaspoon of red powder from one of her kitchen canisters.

"What's that?" asked the Lieutenant doubtfully.

"Chili powder," said Lupe. "Chili is real good for you. That's why there are so many old people around here."

She poured the steaming mixture into a basin on the floor beside the Lieutenant.

"This will take the swelling right out of your foot," she said.

"And the chili powder?" asked the Lieutenant, eyeing the basin.

"Chili is good for curing lots of things," Lupe assured him. "Only you better not get any in your eye. You just soak your foot in this. Then we'll put a poultice on it, and tomorrow you'll feel better."

The Lieutenant obediently lowered one long leg over the side of the couch and did as he was told. Meanwhile, Roberto retrieved the pack they had stashed in Tony's shed, laying out their small store of supplies on the living room floor. Besides the sabotaged radio, there was a first aid kit, a spotting scope, a pair of binoculars with a range finder, and a wind gauge. For weapons they had brought two automatic pistols, an assault rifle, the big .50 caliber Viper, and enough ammunition to keep them in business for a long time.

"For very long ranges, no?" asked Tony, hefting the Viper admiringly.

"For a sharpshooter like the Lieutenant, you wouldn't believe how long," said Roberto proudly.

"So who were you supposed to be shooting at?" asked Tony.

"Emiliano," answered the Lieutenant.

"It's fifty miles to Truchas," said Tony. "This thing can't shoot that far."

"They were going to kill him last night at Fiesta," explained Lupe. "They were guessing he would probably make a speech while everyone was there to see Zozobra."

"They got that right, didn't they?" said Tony. "That little rooster could never resist getting up and making a fool of himself in front of a crowd."

The Lieutenant went on to explain how they had used aerial photographs and Roberto's first hand knowledge of Santa Fe to find one of the big houses in the foothills where they would have a clear shot at the stage from a distance of no more than a mile. A single well-placed shot would have taken care of Emiliano. This would have been followed by mass panic as people began to realize that he had been assassinated. Patrols would have been sent out immediately to search for the killer, but no one would have dreamed of looking for him at such a fantastic distance from the stage. The plan was for them to lie low for a couple of days and then walk back to the highway to rendezvous with their ride back to their base.

The helicopter attack had been added at the last minute. Of course, it was clear now from the sabotaged radio that someone or some group preferred a messy helicopter attack to a single bullet from the Viper. The only question was why.

"But that's all water under the bridge," said the Lieutenant. "Right now we have a new mission to think about. This little girl, what's her name?"

"Paquita," said Father T.J. "And a sweeter child would be hard to find."

"The quicker we get her away from those cabrónes the better," said Lupe.

"I say we intercept them at Tres Piedras," said Roberto. "La Puta's brother used to work up there with the Forest Service. Sometimes he would give me the key to the gate so I could fish the Rio Vallecito. That's real open country up there. Good shooting. And there's bound to be a check point at the intersection of 285 and the road across the gorge from Taos."

"La Puta?" asked the Lieutenant. He had never heard his partner mention anyone by that name.

"My ex-wife," said Roberto with a frown. "Lupe can tell you all about her sometime. They used to be chums."

"In high school," said Lupe hastily. "But I haven't kept track of her."

This was not precisely true. They all knew where Roberto's wife was and what shameful things she was doing.

The year after Tony and Lupe were married, Roberto married a girl who had just as much beauty as Lupe but had far less character. She had taken a job as a waitress in one of the expensive hotels near the Plaza, and within a month, had run off with a high rolling tourist from Las Vegas. Roberto had been crushed by her betrayal, but he did not try to get her back. The separation was final but without the formality of divorce. The girl had simply pulled up stakes and moved to Las Vegas, where she had immediately begun working as a dealer and developed a lucrative sideline as the serial mistress of a dozen middle-aged, middle management casino executives. Everyone said that when her looks finally left her she would return to Santa Fe, but Roberto was not looking forward to that day. He seldom spoke of her at all, but when he did, he referred to her always as "La Puta," The Whore.

"Roberto is right about the country up there," said Tony. "It's flat and open and you can easily see for as far as that thing will shoot."

So it was decided that they would leave as soon as possible and try to take control of that intersection at Tres Piedras before Emiliano and the girl arrived. Coming from Truchas, they would almost certainly cross the Rio Grande at the big suspension bridge on Highway 64. From there it was only a few miles to the intersection where they would be waiting in ambush.

Lupe had been thinking of that moment of confrontation, and she had decided that she needed a weapon. The pistols that the Lieutenant and Roberto had brought with them were of no interest to her, and she went instead to her kitchen drawer. At the back, buried among the can openers and potato peelers was an old ice pick. She wrapped the handle tightly with friction tape and sharpened the point on her whetstone. A good weapon if you were close enough, she thought, and Lupe intended to be very close to Peligro when he died.

29

The same storm that had lightly frosted Santa Fe with white dumped a good three inches of snow on the town of Creed. Two hundred miles farther north and a full two thousand feet higher in altitude, the old mining town woke to find its picturesque streets covered with a foretaste of the conditions that would soon make travel difficult across the whole upper Rio Grande Valley.

Creed was built during the Colorado silver boom. Squeezed into the narrow mouth of a steep sided box canyon, the town was a combination of Victorian charm and spectacular natural beauty. So charming and beautiful was it, in fact, that after the silver boom died out, the area became a popular vacation spot on the strength of its quaint architecture, its stunning scenery, and its nearby trout fishing.

When the Fidelistas began their campaign of terror, the tourists had deserted Creed as fast as they had left Santa Fe, and for several months the future of the little town had looked grim. Then the Patriots had arrived like the cavalry riding to the rescue. They chose the little town as the headquarters of their southern brigade, and the people of Creed welcomed them along with the commerce that they brought with them. Soon young people from all over the region were coming to Creed to join the Patriots.

The first task of the new recruits was to build their own housing. Soon pine log barracks lined the runways of the old airport. A big cafeteria was also built to feed the men and their families as well as an infirmary and a school for the children.

Besides construction work, new recruits took classes in American history, literature, and civics. Their military training was conducted by veterans who were joining up in growing numbers. But their studies came first because Boss Beckwith believed that the more a man knew about the history and culture of the United States of America, the more he would want to defend it.

Because they preached self-reliance and individual responsibility, the Patriots were growing stronger in every part of the West except the coastal regions. They were also responding to a hunger in the population for a way to demonstrate love of country. Patriotism had gone out of fashion in the early years of the twenty first century. Utopian schemes of world government and the smothering embrace of the Nanny State had polluted the pure springs of nationalism that had sustained America's rise to greatness.

The political landscape had also become confused and muddied. The old Liberal/Conservative fault lines had deepened, with the Statists remaining true to their vision of an all-powerful state that promised lifelong care in return for the payment of exorbitant taxes and obedience to a vast number of rules and regulations.

For years the Statists had successfully disguised this quasi-police state as nothing more than a moderately left-wing government that was sincerely concerned about the welfare of the young, the old, and the disadvantaged. However, as the Patriots' growing popularity demonstrated, the people were beginning to understand that the helping hand of big government inevitably became the clenched fist of oppression.

In response to this, the right wing of American politics had splintered into a number of competing parties, each calling for its own brand of minimalist government. However, without political unity there was little chance that any of these plans would ever become anything more than attractive daydreams.

Such political calculations were of little concern to Boss Beckwith, who saw himself as a sort of drill instructor for the whole nation. The debilitating effects of decades of Statist rule were only too obvious to him. People lacked initiative. They were poorly educated. Many were lazy. They simply did as their impulses directed without any attempt to exert self-control or to accept personal responsibility. The whole country, it seemed to him, lacked character, and he had made it his goal to restore as much of that missing character as possible to the young men and women who listened to his radio broadcasts or actually joined his Patriots.

Like any good drill instructor he was up early that morning, despite the exhausting journey of the day before. He had not gotten to bed until after midnight, but he was already standing in line the next morning when the mess hall opened for breakfast.

After downing a double order of scrambled eggs and hash browns, he finished his meal off with a third cup of black coffee and headed for the radio station to record a series of messages that were to be broadcast over the Patriots' powerful short wave radio network.

These broadcasts had proved to be one of the most effective weapons against the Statists. There were shortwave stations all over the West sending out the Patriot message over various frequencies in case the government ever decided to jam their broadcasts base. These stations had all been paid for with the proceeds from cigarette smuggling. Each night a series of broadcasts went out across the United States. These included news and talk shows, stories from American history, and editorials such as the ones that he was about to record. A growing audience listened to these broadcasts with new listeners buying up shortwave radios as fast as they could, despite the heavy excise taxes which the Statists had levied on them.

The radio station was located several miles outside of town at an old guest ranch. The main house stood at the center of a huge meadow and commanded a clear view for several miles in every direction. Every night the crew raised the antenna, powered up the generators, and began broadcasting their four-hour schedule of programs.

When Boss Beckwith arrived he was shown the way to a little studio and given a small tape recorder. He took out his scripts to begin rehearsing them, but before he could key the microphone, the engineer held up a note for him to read through the glass. "Flash!" it said. "This morning's network news shows are reporting that Santa Fe has been attacked and lots of people killed or wounded. What gives?"

A good question thought Boss Beckwith, but one he would think about after he had finished recording his scripts. He smiled at the engineer and waved his hand jauntily as if to say, "Don't worry about it." Then he began to read in the deep rich baritone voice that was loved by millions of Americans.

30

The former President was bored. He was tired of waiting to be shipped off to D.C. to do his little dog and pony show for the media. He had always hated those nosey bastards anyway, even thought most of them were on his side. He wished she would just make the announcement and get it over with, but he could guess the reason for the delay. There must have been objections from the Cabinet. That would have thrown her into a hissy fit. Madam President hated to be crossed by anyone, particularly himself.

He had been watching one of his favorite videos, and now he picked up the phone and dialed the number of an old friend in Washington D.C. who he hadn't called for months.

"Hey there!" he said, making himself comfortable in the big swivel chair behind his desk. "I was just sitting here watching that video you gave me a long time ago. The one of your old girlfriend. Remember?—How could you forget, right?—So, this gal is for real? I mean this isn't some kind of high tech animation is it?—Jesus, she is amazing! I mean, you talk about someone bending over backwards to please!—Yea, Dick, I know, they're taping these calls. They tell me she reads the transcripts too. Hello, Sweetie! I'm just sitting here watching some girl screw this guy sixteen ways from Sunday. Why don't you just tell your little Toy Boy to shove it somewhere else and come on down here and watch it with me?—Wait a minute, Dick! Don't hang up!—OK. No more jokes. I just called to see what the mood is up there.—Well, you know they're flying me up there to say a few words to the media types. Bringing the old magician out of retirement to calm the waters. Anyway, I wanted to get your thinking on what I should say.—Security, Security, Security? Right, and how about the kids? You know, 'A safer world for our children?' That sort of thing? Always worked before.—Right, and the grand kids too. Shit, yes. Keep all the little buggers safe for all I care. After all, I am a grandfather now, you know. Never hurts to bring in a little personal touch. Wait just a minute, while I get some of this down on paper."

He laid the telephone aside and scribbled a few notes on a pad. Then he picked up the phone again. "What happens next, you say? You'll have to ask her, old buddy. She calls the shots. Doesn't let me in on her thinking much these days. Doesn't need the old campaigner now that she's safely into her second term. So it's off to the Ozarks with me, and no goddam visitors either. At least none I can really use, if you catch my drift. She's got the Secret Service in her pocket, and probably up her whatsit too.—By the way, there's a real nice golf course down here in case you ever want to come down and play a round or two with me.—What you say? Got to go? Well, me too, I guess. Pretty busy getting ready for the return. So, I'll see you when I get there, OK? And thanks again for this video."

He put the phone down and looked glumly at the blank screen of the TV monitor. The tape had run out. He looked for a moment at the notes he had made, and then he pushed the rewind button on the VCR and walked across the room to lock the door.

31

PATRIOT RADIO IS ON THE AIR...

Hello out there, my fellow Americans. This is Colonel Dalton Lamar Beckwith of the Patriots, speaking to you from somewhere in the Rockies. Today, I want to talk to you about what you can do as an individual to resist the Statist propagandists who manipulate the attitudes of all those tragically misguided folks who still support them.

Think for a moment how often you have cursed the lies that come spewing out of Atlanta, New York, and Los Angeles. We have all observed how the deck is stacked against us. Statists are never held to account for their misdeeds, while Conservatives are vilified at every turn. If Statists are caught doing wrong, the news is buried on a back page, and our attention is diverted to stories about murder trials or terrorism. If, on the other hand, Conservatives go wrong, the front pages are full of the story for weeks.

The entertainment industry bears its share of the blame too. For decades our movies and TV shows have projected the Statist worldview. Businessmen, preachers and soldiers are portrayed as villains because Statists reject the very concepts of personal responsibility, morality, and discipline which men in those professions embody.

Today's moviemakers think nothing of rewriting history. They paint Statists in the most flattering light and cast Conservatives in dark and ugly tones. Far from being artists, such filmmakers are no better than propagandists, and that is how they should be treated.

But what can we do as individuals to fight these powerful media companies? Simple! We can refuse to buy their product. If your newspaper is full of Statist propaganda, cancel your subscription. If the television news is biased in favor of the Statists, boycott those broadcasts and write to the advertisers to tell them how you feel. If today's movies are nothing but thinly disguised advertising for the Statist point of view, rent yourself some classic films and watch them on your tape deck at home. Let those theater seats go empty and the popcorn grow stale. Don't play their game. If we hit them hard in the pocketbook, even the big multinational corporations will soon get the point.

It's time to stop complaining and start acting. I urge you to consider carefully before you buy another newspaper or magazine or watch another movie or television show. If you enjoy being lied to and manipulated, then give them your money; but if you want to learn to think for yourself, then strike a blow for freedom. Keep your money in your pocket, turn your back on their lies, and leave them with only fools for an audience.

32

Alejandro had awakened with a headache that morning after a night full of ugly surprises. First, the trucks had returned from Santa Fe loaded with wounded and dispirited men instead of the drunken revelers he had expected. He had watched in disbelief as they straggled off to their barracks or tried to tend to the wounded. Worse than that had been the sight of Emiliano himself, wild eyed and acting half crazed as he and Peligro dragged a hysterical young girl toward the radio room.

Alejandro had done what he could. He sent a call to Truchas for medical aid. Then he went to see about the three young men he had personally given leave to attend Fiesta. One had been killed, one was badly wounded, and the third could hardly stammer out what had happened. From him Alejandro learned about Emiliano's speech and the way he had brutalized the young girl standing beside him at the microphone. About the rocket attack he learned very little because the young man was only able to give his disjointed impressions of violent concussions, the screams of the victims, and the smell of burnt flesh.

After he had done a final count of the dead and wounded, he went to report. Emiliano had finished his brief broadcast and was already asleep with Peligro hovering in the shadows like some kind of evil acolyte guarding his master. The girl was lying sideways on top of the covers at the foot of his bed as far away from her tormentor as her tether would allow.

"There are six dead," Alejandro reported.

"Eight," corrected Peligro. "Vincente and his brother took a direct hit. There was not enough left to bring back."

"Five are pretty badly wounded, but I managed to get a doctor."

"Fucking helicopters," spat Peligro. "How I hate those gringos!"

"Why did they do this?"

"Politics," said Peligro contemptuously. "Everything they do is for fucking politics. They worry about winning the next election more than they do about who they kill. Innocent people died tonight for somebody's votes. You can bet on it."

It occurred to Alejandro that Emiliano's car bombs also killed innocent people for an essentially political purpose, but he said only, "What about him?"

"He's all right," asserted Peligro. "He just needs a little rest."

"And the girl?"

Peligro smiled, showing his uneven teeth. "Isn't she something? You ought to see her, Bro. She's got tits like a centerfold. No lie."

"I heard he had her up on stage, feeling her up just before the attack."

Peligro smiled even more broadly. "He's a genius about things like that, Bro. He is showing them who is boss. See? He gets the girl up there, and he plays with her tits, and there is nothing they can do to stop him because no one has the cojones to try. He is rubbing their noses in it, no? Shaming them, so they don't start thinking they are heroes or something. If he wants to feel her tits, he does it. If he wants to take her to Creed and give her to Boss Beckwith, he does it. He does what he wants, and all they can do is watch."

Alejandro said nothing. He had been taught to respect women, and the thought of Emiliano pawing at this slip of a girl in front of hundreds of people turned his stomach.

"She seems to be in pretty bad shape," he said. "Maybe she should sleep somewhere else."

"Like your bed?" laughed Peligro. "Nice try, Bro. She is for Emiliano only, but you can have her little brother if you want someone to warm your bed. He is very high spirited."

Peligro turned the lamp so that light shown into a dark corner of the room. For the first time Alejandro saw a boy lying there. He was trussed up with duct tape. A blindfold and gag covered most of his face, and he was unconscious.

"This one is a tough little rooster," said Peligro. "He climbed up in our truck to get his sister. He was kicking and punching everyone so we had to knock him out a little, but he is stronger than he looks, so be careful when he wakes up."

Alejandro decided that if he could not help the girl, at least he could do something for the unconscious boy, so he carried him to his quarters and deposited him on his narrow bed. Then he untied him, removed the blind fold and gag, and turned up the light to examine the boy's injuries.

It was then that he discovered the last little joke that fate had to play on him that night for as he looked closer, he realized with a shock that the boy in his bed was Joselito Vigil, his first cousin on his mother's side of their vast extended family. Worse than that, if this was Joselito, then the girl lying bound hand and foot in Emiliano's bed must be his pretty little cousin Paquita, whom he, Alejandro, would be honor bound to defend.

"Joselito," he said, "It's me. Your cousin Alejandro."

"The boy shook his head to clear the grogginess."

"Cousin?"

"I was at your grandmother's funeral and your sister's first communion."

"Mother said you had gone over to the Fidelistas," said the boy with disgust.

"I am trying to get back our land," said Alejandro defensively. "The Vigil grant. It is yours too, you know."

"And you stole Paquita."

"Not me."

"She is here," the boy insisted. "With that pig."

"Yes."

"Then help me."

"I will."

"OK. Let's go."

"Wait, Joselito. It's not that easy. She is still with Emiliano."

"I don't care. I have to take her home."

"You will, but for now you have to wait."

He extracted a solemn promise from the boy to stay where he was until he returned. Then he locked him in and hurried out to see what he could do about dispersing some of the men in case there was a second attack on the camp itself. What the Americans might do next he could not say. He had enough on his mind to try and map out his own next move.

33

Esmeralda had not been so loaded down since Fr. T.J. had taken his Sunday school group on a ski trip many years before. Six rowdy teens along with their skis, boots, jackets and snacks had been quite a load for the old van then, but it was nothing compared to the burden she was being asked to carry now. Besides the five adults, she was loaded down with weapons, ammunition, spare tires, jerry cans full of gasoline and Father T.J.'s idea of a three-day supply of food. Still, the old van did her best, wallowing along from pothole to pothole as she headed north out of Santa Fe along old U.S. 285.

The first check point was just beyond the padlocked entrance to the deserted Santa Fe Opera. The barricades marked the boundary of Pueblo land and had been in place since the beginning of the conflict. For the next fifteen miles the highway passed through both the Tesuque and Pojoaque pueblos. No stopping was allowed along that stretch and vehicles were checked upon entering and leaving the area in order to make sure that none of the ugly little war found its way onto Pueblo land.

Early in the conflict the people of all twenty-four Pueblos had counseled among themselves and decided they wanted no part of Emiliano's so-called reconquest of America. Their main concern, as always, was to defend their land and protect their culture from being corrupted by outsiders. In this instance as in others they followed the example of their ancient ancestors, pulling up their ladders behind them, as it were, and shutting off contact with the outside world.

There were precious few Fidelista sympathizers among the Pueblo People and fewer still of the greedy sort who might wish for the return of the tourists with their bulging wallets and ever-present cameras. They were content to follow the example of their brother the tortoise, from whom they had learned the art of surviving under difficult conditions.

The tortoise lives for many years despite long droughts and freezing winters. He is not swift and he is not fierce. He does not draw attention to himself like the magpie or move about restlessly like the jackrabbit. He lives quietly and bothers no one. When danger threatens he simply withdraws into his shell. The tortoise leads a simple life but a long one, and by following his example, the Pueblo people had managed to maintain their unique culture for many centuries. They had not been defeated by the attacks of the plains tribes or totally converted by the missionary zeal of the Spanish priests. Even more miraculous, they had not been entirely seduced by the technology of the modern world. The way of the tortoise had protected them many times before, and they hoped it would save them once again.

Father T.J. pulled up to the barricade and waited.

"What have we got here?" asked Lieutenant McDowell from the back seat. He was sitting with his rapidly improving foot supported on top of a knapsack full of water bottles and his pistol within easy reach under his right hip.

"Tesuque check point," said Tony. "Don't worry. They're strictly neutral."

Two Tesuque men were sitting in the shade of a cottonwood tree. On the weather beaten picnic table between them lay a two-way radio and a lever action deer rifle. The younger of the two got up and strolled toward the van. He was smiling broadly.

"Nice to see you and Esmeralda again, Father T.J."

It was Henry Red Wing. He had worked for several years as a guard at the Palace of the Governors in Santa Fe, but his friendship with Father T.J. and Tony dated from the summers they had spent together umpiring youth league softball games.

He leaned down to look inside the van, resting his forearms on the roof above the window. He was still smiling, but his eyes took in everything, and Father T.J. was glad that they had taken the time to conceal the weapons.

"Hello, Tony. Nice to see you and the wife again," said the young Tesuque man.

"I guess you heard about the attack," said Tony.

"We heard the explosions," said Henry, "but we just thought it was the usual fireworks. Then someone heard Emiliano's little tirade on the radio. Was it really that bad?"

"Don't know. We weren't there," said Tony.

This was technically true, of course, but Tony could not help feeling that he had just told his old friend a bald-faced lie.

"Headed north, I see," said Red Wing, hoping for more information about what his friends were up to.

"A little way," said Father T.J. He was no more comfortable with half-truths than Tony.

Henry Red Wing could see they were acting strangely. Still, he did not ask about the two men in the back of the van. Judging by his haircut, the tall young Anglo was probably a soldier, though certainly not a Fidelista. Still, who he was and what he might be doing in the company of his friends was no longer any of Henry's business. That was how neutrality worked.

"Be careful you don't run into Emiliano and his bunch," he said. "According to the radio he is heading north too, and that guy is bad medicine."

"We'll be careful," said Father T.J.

Suddenly it occurred to Henry Red Wing that the two strangers might actually be kidnapping his friends. Just in case, he decided to give Father T.J. an excuse to get out of the van.

"If you'll just step over here and sign the visitors list, you can be on your way, Father T.J.," he said, stepping back and opening the van door.

"Visitors list?"

"Yes, if you'll just come this way, please."

Father T.J. followed Henry Red Wing to the picnic table, where the Tesuque man handed him a blank piece of notebook paper.

"Just sign that," said Henry Red Wing. "Write down the number of people in your party."

"What's this all about, Henry?"

"Just keep writing and don't look back at the van."

Father T.J. was momentarily mystified, but he did as he was told.

"Those men," said Henry Red Wing, "are they holding you all hostage or something?"

Father T.J. laughed. "You think we're being kidnapped?"

"Just trying to look out for old friends."

"I appreciate your concern, Henry. But no, we are not being kidnapped."

"Well, if you are determined to go north, just be careful. There's something I haven't told you about this Emiliano guy."

"Yes?"

"You know how some of our old ones believe he is a shape-changer?"

"Surely you don't believe that, Henry. That's nothing but superstition. People may act a little like animals, but they don't actually change into them."

"Listen to me, Father. One morning last month I was walking down by the river looking for beaver sign, but I found something else instead. Something I didn't like at all."

"And what was that, my friend?"

"A big track! Father T.J. 'This big!'" He held up his hands as if cupping a small saucer between them. "It was either the biggest cougar I ever saw or it was something else."

"And what could that be?"

"Remember the story that Tony tells about his great grandfather killing a big jaguar up near Truchas?"

"You think a jaguar made that track?"

"What better spirit for such an evil man to take than the spirit of a Mexican jaguar?"

Father T.J. looked displeased.

"I'm sorry, Father," said Henry Red Wing. "I'm just telling you what the old ones are thinking. They would tell you to stay away from anything that has to do with Emiliano."

"Good advice, no doubt."

"Good advice. But you're not going to take it. Right?"

"There is something we must do, my friend. Later perhaps, I will explain. But for now, I thank you for your concern."

"Will you at least take this with you for friendship's sake?"

Henry Red Wing reached into his pocket and handed the priest a small stone fetish carved in the shape of a bear.

"More superstition!" said Father T.J. gruffly, unable to conceal his pleasure at receiving such a gift.

"As a favor, Father. I would feel better if you had that with you."

Father T.J. slipped the fetish into his shirt pocket, and the two men returned to the van. Henry Red Wing unlatched the barrier and moved it out of their path.

"OK then," he said. "You know the rules. No stopping till you get to the Pojoaque checkpoint. If you don't show up there on time, we'll send someone out to look for you."

Father T.J. started the van and Henry Red Wing waved them through. "You folks have a nice day," he said in his best museum guard manner and Esmeralda lurched forward, heading north toward the unknown.

34

"Oh, Cho Cho. Don't stop!" the President pleaded.

Cho Lin Wok looked down at the President of the United States, her skirt pushed up around her waist, her legs clutching around his thrusting hips. As usual she was begging for more, but lately it was all he could do to give her even this small portion of what she demanded. There were just too many distractions. For instance, this particular sofa always developed an annoying squeak when their exertions reached a critical point. He could never avoid the panicky feeling that they were being overheard, even though he knew that this was probably the most secure room on earth. It was scanned for listening devices every morning and was designed to be completely soundproof as well as bulletproof. Still, he could not help worrying, especially when she began the crescendo of sighs, squeals, and finally screams that always accompanied her climax. It took all the self-control that his Buddhist training had taught him to be able to maintain even a passable erection while making love to the President in the Oval Office.

As usual she did not try to hide her disappointment.

"So soon?" she moaned. "Oh, more, Cho Cho. More."

"You need a regiment, like Catherine the Great had," he laughed.

"Don't be cross," she said coquettishly. "I just want you all the time. I can't stand being without you for more than a day or two."

More like an hour or two, thought Wok. Hadn't the last time been just a few hours ago after the Cabinet meeting? Or was his memory failing him too?

She reached up and ran a finger along his almost hairless cheek.

"You're so young," she said. "So strong. I know you can do anything, Cho Cho. But for now just kiss me and call me by our secret name, and I won't bother you any more."

"You're not bothering me, Madam President," he said, remembering too late that she hated to be called Madam President while they were making love.

Her anger was instantaneous and breathtaking in its ferocity. "For shit's sake," she screeched, pushing him away. "Don't give me that Madam President crap! You know damn good and well what I want you call me."

Quickly he bent down and breathed in her ear. "You are my little Lotus," he whispered. "My beautiful little Lotus."

"Now isn't that better?" she murmured, offering her neck to be kissed.

Luckily for Wok the President was completely unaware that their pet name was really his private little joke. In his mind he was comparing her, not to the delicate flower, but rather to the powerful little sports car by the same name. This seemed to him a far better metaphor for the formidable woman who was just now giving him a long, penetrating kiss. Like a classic Lotus, she was good looking in spite of her age, responsive to the slightest touch, and quick to reach top speed. As if to prove his little joke, he took her for a short test drive, caressing her nipples to little peaks and reaching down to press her accelerator. She began to shudder at his touch.

"Don't get me started," she said, pulling away. "You're all through, remember?"

"For the moment, my dear," he replied with transparent bravado.

Secretly he hoped it would be quite a long moment indeed for, to continue the automotive metaphor, he knew he was running on empty.

Suddenly she was all business. She sat up abruptly and adjusted her clothing.

"There's something I want you to do, Cho Cho," she said, walking over to the big desk. She scribbled something on a piece of paper and handed it to him.

"This is the name and address of one of the women my husband was screwing before we shipped him off to Arkansas. I want you to make sure she is on the plane with him tomorrow. Tell her she's a sort of welcome home present from the Secret Service. Tell her anything, but get her on that plane. Do you understand?"

"A welcome home present?" said Wok.

"You might call it that," she said. "Just make sure she's on that plane."

35

After he finished recording his message, Colonel Beckwith picked up the latest news bulletins from the radio room. He scanned through them quickly to see what they said about his supposed attack on Santa Fe. There were only two small stories on the wire. The first reported the attack and gave estimates of the casualties. The second blamed it all on his Patriots. Both stories were attributed to "informed sources." It was an old trick of theirs, doctoring the news to make his Patriots seem like something more than they actually were, but they had carried it to an extreme in this case. If the reports of the attack were true, and all those people had been killed then it must have been carried out by professionals. The Fidelistas certainly wouldn't attack themselves, and that left the U.S. Army as the only force in the region capable of launching such a raid. But why would the U.S. Army be attacking a city full of innocent civilians?

Another story that caught his eye was about the murder of the senator from Wyoming. He had been gunned down in an apparent drive-by shooting outside his Georgetown apartment. Beckwith had met the senator once at a barbecue his Patriots had sponsored to raise funds for conservative candidates. He approved of the way the man had spoken up for the old values, and Beckwith was sorry to see him pass from the scene. He determined to do a profile on the late senator for one of his broadcasts. He was just beginning to jot down some ideas for the piece when the TV, which was kept tuned to the CCN satellite link, began to flash its "Breaking News" logo. Beckwith put down his pencil and listened.

"Last night forces of the right wing paramilitary organization known as The Patriots launched a rocket attack against Fidelista guerillas who were attending the famous Santa Fe Fiesta. The attackers fired rockets into the huge crowd, which was attending the opening ceremonies at Ft. Marcy Park. Unconfirmed reports place the number of casualties at more than twenty-five dead with two hundred or more wounded. It is not known how many of the dead and wounded were Fidelistas and how many were innocent men, women, and children. Experts on terrorism say that such a bloody attack by this renegade militia group with ties to the Klu Klux Klan may indicate an intensification and a widening of the war in the West. More details when they become available."

"...a widening of the war in the West..." The words rang in Beckwith's brain like an air raid siren. He was on his feet in an instant heading for his car. If the U.S. military could attack Santa Fe and blame it on his Patriots, they might just as likely attack Creed and blame it on the Fidelistas.

So far, there had been no confrontations between the Patriots and the Fidelistas. Beckwith had judged that it was all to the good to have the U.S. Army fighting a two front war. War was not really the word for what had been going on between his Patriots and the U.S. Army. All their confrontations had been kept at a low boil with nothing more than a few relatively minor skirmishes to disturb the peace.

Patriot forces had acted only to interfere with the enforcement of those laws that self-reliant Westerners despised. Coercive regulations which limited the rights of landowners and placed the dictates of bureaucrats in Washington D.C. above the will of local people were simply ignored wherever the Patriots held sway. Most Westerners supported Boss Beckwith and his followers, seeing them as nothing more than a healthy response to the heavy taxes and foolish laws that had been foisted on them over the years by Statist politicians.

Having won the hearts and minds of the people, the Patriots had contented themselves with propaganda efforts to increase their numbers. Sometimes a small detachment of troops would be sent out to reassert the authority of the Statists in one locale or another, but after a skirmish or two, they would withdraw, never mounting a real offensive that might have done away with the Patriots for good. Boss Beckwith believed this was because the ranks of the U.S. Army were full of men who were Patriot sympathizers and the higher-ups were afraid of a rebellion among their own troops.

Now, however, this rocket attack on Santa Fe seemed to be signaling a shift in strategy. He knew that CCN had always been the propaganda arm of the Statists, and he did not take their words lightly. *"A widening war in the West"* indeed. All right, so be it. He had always known it would come to that eventually, but he wondered if his men were really ready for it.

As he drove toward town, he contacted the base commander by radio.

"Captain Fellows? Beckwith here. Go to yellow alert immediately. Cancel the inspection and begin sending the men and their families to the shelters at once. I'll explain why when I get there."

36

Emiliano awoke, feeling no better after a long and exhausted sleep. He had been dreaming of the treasure trove of Navajo jewelry that was waiting for him, buried deep in the deserted sculpture garden at Shidoni. In his dream he had dug it up and spread it all out on the grass where he could admire it in the light of day. The heavy silver necklaces and concho belts gleamed like the chrome on a new Cadillac and the jewelry from the homes of the rich and famous sparkled in the sun. He had hidden it well, and he was sure that it would still be waiting for him one day when he went back to dig it up. One day he would cash in those jewels and that silver and use it to buy the good life on a Cuban beach far away from all this death and destruction.

Emiliano was still completely undone by the shock he had suffered the night before. He was now more certain than ever that he was not the dull and dimwitted sort of fellow who could endure such an assault on his sensibilities without serious psychological consequences, and he lay there for a few moments, enjoying an ecstasy of self-pity. Then he reached for the girl to pull her close, and found to his consternation that she was gone.

The rope that had bound her hands still lay at the foot of the bed, but she was nowhere to be seen. This discovery brought Emiliano to his feet. He stumbled into his clothes and went out into the morning sun to look for her. The brilliant light stopped him in his tracks just beyond his own doorway. He shielded his sleep-crusted eyes to ward it off, and spoke to the guard who had been posted beside his door.

"Where is the girl?" he croaked.

"She is with Alejandro, Jefe."

"Alejandro?"

"Sí, Jefe. After Peligro went to get your car ready, Alejandro came to see about the girl. He took her to the latrine to get washed up."

Emiliano's legs suddenly seemed to be working over time just to hold him up, so he sat down on a nearby bench to wait for them to become fully operational.

"They say Peligro saved your life, Jefe. Is that true?"

Emiliano's memory of the rocket attack was still vague. He remembered the noise of the explosions and Peligro's comforting weight pressing him down to safety. He remembered the screams of the people and the familiar smell of high explosives mixing with the earthy smell of the adobe bricks pressed next to his face. And he remembered the caress of the girl's wonderful black hair.

"Yes," said Emiliano. "Peligro was very loyal."

"Are you feeling all right, Jefe?"

"Yes, of course. You don't need to hover around like that. Just go and find Alejandro and the girl and bring them to me."

The guard hurried off, and Emiliano leaned back and closed his eyes. He tried to make some sense out of the situation. They had attacked him with helicopters. But what were they planning to do next? If the Yankees were going to start playing rough, then an alliance with the Patriots was even more important. In his mind that made the girl more important too.

When his legs felt stronger, he went back inside to wash his face and find a cigar to chew on. He emerged to find Alejandro and the girl coming across the dusty parade ground in his direction. The boy who had given so much trouble the night before was also with them as well as a sizeable group of Fidelistas who were hoping for a repeat of last night's performance with the girl.

"Who told you that you could untie those two, Alejandro?" said Emiliano sternly.

"There is something you should know, Jefe," replied Alejandro. "These children are my cousins, Joselito and Paquita, from La Ciénega."

He watched Emiliano closely to see if he grasped the full importance of what he was being told.

"Your cousins?" croaked Emiliano.

"Their mother is my aunt Josephina. That means I am responsible for them, Jefe."

"I see," said Emiliano.

The situation had rapidly escalated from a minor problem to a serious one. Emiliano understood that by dishonoring this slip of a girl he had also dishonored Alejandro. He knew that such offenses were not taken lightly by these people from the old extended families that had populated these mountains for centuries. In fact, this was precisely the reason why he had taken such liberties with the girl in the first place. The worse the offense, the more powerful his domination over them became. But the fact that this girl was a blood cousin to one of his lieutenants was a very different thing. He knew that Alejandro could never forgive what he had done to her or the boy, and he cursed the fate that had guided Peligro's eye toward this particular girl.

"Did you hear me, Jefe?" repeated Alejandro, this time with a slight edge to his voice. "I am responsible for this girl. I cannot let you take her to Creed."

Now it was out in the open. A direct challenge to his authority. The others had heard, and they were watching intently to see how he would handle this minor mutiny. Emiliano was sad to think of what might be required of him now. He noted that Alejandro was wearing his pistol, but that he had not unsnapped the flap on the holster. His own holster had no flap, and since he used a revolver and Alejandro carried an automatic with no shell in the chamber, he knew that he would be able to get off the first shot. From this range he could not miss, but some men were hard to kill and Alejandro might return fire. The sun was in Alejandro's eyes, giving him another slight advantage, but it was not enough to bet his life on.

He hesitated. The men had begun to separate into two camps according to their sympathies. Some stood with Alejandro while others, mostly the men who had come up from Mexico, stood with him.

Emiliano knew that a false move at this point might result in a confrontation that could cost as many lives as last night's attack, so he crossed his arms calmly and took a deep breath. By moving his hand deliberately away from his pistol, he was retreating one small step from the brink of the chasm that had suddenly opened up between the two groups of men.

Just then Peligro came hurrying toward them. He was the last person Emiliano wanted to see at that moment because his quick temper might shove them all over the edge.

"¿Qué pasa?" he asked. "What's going on?"

"This girl you brought here tied up like a prisoner is my cousin," said Alejandro.

Peligro sensed the tension. He squared up to the men who were standing with Alejandro and began choosing his targets. The chasm yawned even wider.

"Then you probably don't want her to go to Creed with us," said Peligro flashing a broad smile which was enough to send two or three of the men scuttling for the sidelines.

"I am responsible for her safety," repeated Alejandro grimly.

"So what do you think we should do about that, Jefe?" said Peligro, not taking his smile off the men standing with Alejandro.

"I think we need to talk about it," said Emiliano. "But not here."

"I want to talk about it here and now," insisted Alejandro, who had been emboldened by the number of men who had taken his side. "She is my cousin, and I have the right to decide what is best for her." His own hand now hovered dangerously close to his holster. "These two young ones have told me how you behaved with her at Fiesta," he added in words that rasped out between his teeth. "That was no way to treat a young girl!"

Emiliano knew that Peligro might make his move at any moment. Desperately he searched for words that would put a stop to the deadly spiral of machismo that threatened to engulf them all. The awful urgency of the moment rendered him speechless, but then another voice, as surprising as it was commanding, spoke up.

"Wait!"

It was Paquita. For herself she no longer cared, but her brother was standing next to Alejandro looking as belligerent as a boy of his age can look, and she was quite sure that he would be killed in the gunfight that was threatening to break out.

"Wait," she repeated. "I will go to Creed with this man. I will go of my own choice, without being tied up." And before anyone could stop her, she stepped across the space between the two groups and stood beside Emiliano.

"Joselito, come with me!" she commanded. "We will wait inside."

She took her brother by the hand and led him away from the flash point.

For a moment the men remained frozen in their combative poses, and then someone laughed.

"Ayee!" one man said. "That one has cojones as big as apples."

"As big as watermelons!" said another.

"Be careful when you grab that one, Jefe. She may grab you back where it hurts the most."

Emiliano laughed along with his men. The moment of death had passed them by, and the chasm healed itself as quickly as it had formed. For a moment he had lost control of the situation, and a deadly revolt had broken out right under his nose. It was just as disturbing to his psyche as the rocket attack had been. Of course, he blamed it all on those proud Spaniards, as they insisted on calling themselves, with their iron clad codes of conduct and their family ties. But it was over now and time to take command again. He turned to Alejandro.

"You go and make sure those cousins of yours are not getting into mischief in my quarters. I want to talk to you privately."

Then he turned to Peligro. "Is the car ready?"

"It was giving some trouble, but it is ready now."

"If the Yankees are coming after us with helicopters, it is even more important for us to talk to these Patriots. Understand?"

"I understand."

"That little excitement made me hungry. Go and get us some food while I talk to the family man."

"I am sorry I chose such a troublesome girl, Jefe. But how could I know?"

"It is not your fault, my friend. Alejandro is the one who is making trouble and now I will put an end to it."

Alejandro was tending the fire in the little corner fireplace when Emiliano returned. The two youngsters were sitting on the bed. Paquita had found a blanket and wrapped it around her shoulders, but she was still shivering as much from the release of tension as from the chill in the room.

"All right," said Emiliano, "this is how it will be. The girl goes with me. And, you take the boy back to his family."

"I'm not leaving without Paquita," said the boy loudly.

"Silence!" shouted Emiliano. "You will do as you are told."

Paquita had not lost her nerve. "Listen, Joselito," she pleaded. "You must go back and take care of our mother. I will be all right." She looked boldly at Emiliano, daring him not to guarantee her safety.

"No one is going to hurt your sister. I promise that," responded Emiliano obediently.

"How can we be sure?" said Alejandro.

"Listen to me, old friend," said Emiliano in a tone that did not quite ring true. "I need an alliance. The girl must go to Creed as we planned. She will be no good to anyone if she is injured, and I promise to treat her as I would treat my own daughter now that I know she is your cousin."

Alejandro hesitated, thinking that Emiliano would probably have prostituted his own daughter if it would further his ambitions.

"Do as I say. Take this boy back to his mother where he belongs. I will give you a pickup to use."

The mention of the word "pickup" opened a new world of possibilities in Alejandro's mind. With a truck he could go anywhere, do anything. For the first time he actually thought about leaving the Fidelistas. He saw clearly now that his real loyalty was to his family not to this bunch of mojados he had been living with. How could he have been so blind not to see that before? Emiliano's men, men he had thought of as his compadres, had turned on him in an instant. Worst of all, he was sure that Peligro would not have hesitated to shoot him where he stood if the girl had not intervened. Men like that could never be trusted again. He would take the truck that Emiliano was offering. He would take Joselito back to La Ciénega and never return to the Fidelistas. As for Paquita, he knew there were other men in the mountain villages who felt as he did about protecting their women. They called themselves The Brotherhood, and from their reputation he knew that if he could just get word to them about what had been done to his cousin and where she was being taken, she would have all the protection she needed on the road to Creed.

37

It was late afternoon in the Ozarks. The former President was rummaging through the top drawer of his dresser looking for his favorite pair of cuff links. They were solid gold, each in the shape of a plump drumstick to remind him of the Chicken King, who had given them to him during his first term as governor. Back then, hundreds of thousands of dollars worth of payoffs had insured that the Chicken King would be allowed to pollute some of the prettiest streams in the state with the waste from millions of chickens. Other men were attracted to the scent of corruption like vultures to carrion, and before long industries were moving to his state in record numbers, and he was receiving so many envelopes stuffed full of cash that his wife had opened a Swiss bank account to hold all the loot. Unfortunately, that huge pile of money wasn't doing them much good now, since his wife had gone power mad and shipped him off to the Ozarks where he couldn't get his hands on it. At least his daughter was getting some fun out of it, he thought, living it up on the Riviera, buzzing around Europe in her bright red Porche on the arm of her latest boy friend, Crown Prince What's His Name.

"Mr. President?" It was Norton, tapping gently on his open door.

"Norton, have you seen my lucky cufflinks?"

"Your drumsticks, sir? No, I haven't."

"Well, Shit! I wanted to take them to D.C. with me, Norton. Goddam it!"

Norton hated the way the old man cursed. It was embarrassing, especially just now when he was trying to introduce the new security man to him

"This is Agent Mathison, Sir. Just down from D.C."

Behind Norton stood a serious looking young man. The former President smiled.

"Sent you down here to guard the old folks home, did they, son?"

"I'll be making sure you get safely on the plane tomorrow, sir."

"Not flying with me?"

"No sir. Someone else will take over when you arrive at Dulles."

"What about you, Norton?"

"I'm staying behind to close up, Mr. President."

"Lock it up good, Norton. Lock it up and throw away the key, by God. I hope I never see this place again."

He turned back to his sock drawer and resumed the search for his cuff links.

Norton stepped forward and handed him a sheaf of papers. "Here's the advance copy of your speech, sir. The White House just faxed it to us."

"Thank you, Norton. It's about time they got that to me. Do they think I can give a performance like this without a little rehearsal?" He put the manuscript on his desk and fished a long red pencil out of his pencil holder. Then he looked back at the newcomer. "Welcome to the Ozarks, Mr. Mathison. Hope you enjoy your stay."

As the door closed softly behind his visitors, he began to read the speech. The working title was "Security for Americans." He scratched that out and wrote "Security for Lazy Butts" above it. That was more like it, he thought. Amazing how no-account people had become these days. Shiftless and stupid too. Nowadays people were only too willing to let someone else do the work for them. All you had to do was to plant a few dozen stories about homelessness or hungry kids in the media, and pretty soon everyone would start clamoring for the government to do something about the problem so they could go back to watching their sitcoms with a clean conscience. Never thought of doing anything about it themselves. Just sat there like bumps on a log waiting for the government to fix things.

Of course, the Statists were only too happy to create yet another program to try and do just that. What did it matter that the programs they devised never seemed to work like they were intended? The people seemed to be willing to pay the extra taxes as long as they thought the rich were getting soaked worse than they were and as long as they didn't have to actually do anything about the problem themselves. If you just took their money and went away quietly, they were happy as pigs in slop. The networks helped keep them that way by feeding them a constant stream of sensational stories about celebrity murders or natural disasters. Soon the people would forget about the homeless and the hungry, assuming everything had been taken care of, but whether it had or not, the taxes and the programs they funded would go on forever.

A nation of nincompoops with short attention spans! That's what they were dealing with, he thought, and so far those nincompoops had let them get away with every scam they had tried. But this was the granddaddy of all scams, so big that it made his palms sweat.

This time they were selling security. They had been leading up to it for months. A few riots, plenty of labor violence, some orchestrated student protests on the college campuses added just the right note of uncertainty to a nation where the Fidelistas were trying to take over the Southwest and the Patriots were pounding their chests every night on the radio. Mix in a little media hysteria and Bingo, you had everyone in the country worrying about his family's security.

It was all her idea, of course. He freely admitted that the best ideas always came from that clever little brain of hers. But this one topped them all. He could hardly believe what she was proposing when she first explained the scheme to him. The sheer audacity of it left him gasping. The two of them had not lived as man and wife for many years, and love was no longer even a memory, but as a colleague and a master politician, she had no equal.

He could see her deft touch in the draft of the speech they had sent him. It was a good speech, but it needed that special tone of sincerity that only he could give it. He was sure the nincompoops would take the bait.

He opened the top drawer of his desk to get an envelope for the manuscript, and there, nested among the paper clips, he found his drumsticks. Things were looking up, he decided. A nationally televised speech, a chance to get back to D.C., and now he had found his good luck charm. It was a good omen, indeed.

38

"Pull over somewhere along here," said the Lieutenant, "before they can see us coming."

They were one hundred miles farther north, approaching the deserted village of Tres Piedras and the intersection of U.S. 285 and N.M. 64, where they expected to find the first Fidelista check point.

Father T.J. did as he was instructed, stopping where the road curved before heading down a long hill into Tres Piedras. They all got out and stretched, grateful that the bumpy ride was over.

"Roberto and I had better walk on ahead a little ways and check things out," said the Lieutenant.

"Do you really feel like walking on that foot?" asked Lupe.

The Lieutenant tested his still swollen foot. "I hope so, ma'am. It's feeling a lot better now, like you said it would."

Roberto had the Viper slung over his shoulder and he was carrying his spotting scope and one of the assault rifles. He handed the big ammunition belt to the Lieutenant.

"This part is our job," said the Lieutenant. "We'll secure the intersection and when it's safe for you all to join us, we'll fire three pistol shots."

"That's three quick shots, like this," said Roberto, pointing an imaginary pistol toward the sky. "Bang! Bang! Bang!"

"Don't come unless you hear that signal," cautioned the Lieutenant. "There may be some other firing, but you all just wait for that signal."

Father T.J. looked slightly pained. "When you say you are going to secure the intersection, you mean…"

"He means we are gonna eliminate any Fidelistas we find there," said Roberto.

"And that's necessary? You couldn't just tie them up or something?"

"I'm afraid not," said the Lieutenant.

"We are lucky to have these two young men to help us," said Lupe. "I think we can depend on them to do what they think is best."

"Well, at least I'd like to say a prayer before they go," said the priest.

He motioned for them all to join hands. Lupe made sure the Lieutenant was part of the circle. Then the priest began talking in a quiet voice, as if God Himself were standing there with them.

"Oh Lord, we pray for the men we may be about to attack. These are men we do not know. Men we do not hate. But men our young friend here says he must kill if we are to save Paquita. We know that it is you alone who have brought these two young soldiers here to help us, and now we ask that you steady their hands and give them the courage to do your will. In the name of your Son, our Savior, Jesus Christ. Amen."

Lieutenant Sandy McDowell had never before thought of himself as an instrument of God's will, but the priest's words reminded him of the enormity of what he was about to do. This was the moment for which he had trained, and the moment, which he had secretly dreaded. He knew that it was his job to kill and to kill well, and though he might have the blessing of this priest, he was still not sure how he would react when it was time to pull the trigger.

"We'd better get going while we still have the light," said Roberto.

The Lieutenant roused himself from thought. "OK then!" he said. "You all wait for the signal. It shouldn't be too long."

The two men hurried up the road, as fast as the Lieutenant's hobbling gait would allow. Just around the curve they came to a place where they could see the checkpoint nearly a mile down the road. A crude barricade draped with the new flag of the People's Republic of Mexico blocked the intersection. Nearby, three armed men lounged beside a battered old Humvee in the driveway of a deserted Dairy Queen. Smoke from their fire curled into the endless blue sky, giving a perfect reading on the afternoon breeze.

"Let's see if we can't get a little closer," said the Lieutenant.

"We can get right up their noses if you want," said the Corporal. "There's plenty of cover."

"Let's paint up first," said the Lieutenant, handing a tube of grease paint to his partner.

So far, it was like a turkey hunt, he thought. First the camouflage, then the stalk, and finally the shot. In this case there would need to be three shots, and that was what worried him. After the first man was down, there was no telling how the other two would react. If one of them reached cover before he could get a shot at him, they would have a heck of a time smoking him out.

They slipped off the road into the brush and moved forward cautiously until they were only about five hundred yards from their targets. There the Lieutenant called a halt..

"This is plenty close enough," he said.

"Wind's in our face," said the Corporal. "That's good."

He handed the Viper to the Lieutenant and set up his own spotting scope.

"Range?" asked the Lieutenant, assuming a prone position so that he could fire from beneath the lower branches of a small juniper.

The Corporal consulted his range finder. "Five hundred and twenty-six, sir."

"These guys are going to run like rabbits after the first shot," said the Lieutenant, sharing his worries.

"If one of them makes it behind that Humvee he'll be tough to dig out."

"Just what I've been thinking."

"So what do you think?"

"How about taking out two with one shot?"

Roberto laughed. "And just how do you plan to do that?"

"One of them steps in front of the other one, see? So they're lined up, right? An AP round from this close would walk right through both of them."

Roberto whistled softly. "That's the kind of shot they tell stories about, sir."

"I wasn't thinking about making a reputation, Corporal. I was just trying to figure how to do this without getting us both killed."

"You really think you can do it?"

"With your help."

"No problem. Just tell me what to do."

"OK. This will be a timing shot, right? I'll zero in on one of the men, and you give me a count when another guy is about to walk in front of him. You just lead him like you would a duck or something."

"That kind of crossover may not happen right away, sir. We can't just make these guys go where we want them to."

"Maybe we'll get lucky, Corporal. If we start to lose shooting light we'll think of something else, but let's try this for a while."

Both men turned back to their telescopes. Their targets looked bored. A big man with a large mustache was talking to another Fidelista, who was leaning against the Humvee, while a boy of about eighteen sat on a log beside the fire, dozing. The Lieutenant decided to take the boy out last. He would probably be the slowest to react and the least trouble to dislodge if he made it to cover. Probably a headshot on the boy, he thought. That way they would have at least one clean uniform to help lure Emiliano into a trap, and that way it was even more like hunting turkeys. Headshots saved the meat.

"Corporal, what is the word for turkey in Spanish?"

"Turkey, sir? It's an Indian word, actually, sir. Guajalote."

"Waha what?"

"Guajalote, sir. Why do you ask?"

"I was just thinking that this is a lot like hunting turkeys. When I was a boy, we always went out and got our own turkey for Thanksgiving or Christmas. My Dad said store-bought turkeys were pumped full of too many chemicals. He said the wild variety was better even if they were a little tough to chew sometimes."

Roberto tapped him on the shoulder. "Check it out, sir," he said excitedly. "Looks like Mr. Mustache is getting restless."

"Go take a leak, buddy," urged the Lieutenant. "You need to take a leak bad."

"He's doing it, sir! Just like you said."

"OK, Corporal, when he comes back, give me a count if he's going to cross in front of the guy leaning on the Humvee. I'm lining up on him, chest high.

I won't be looking at Mr. Mustache at all, so you keep me posted. Nice and smooth now."

"Got it."

Mr. Mustache walked to the side of the road and urinated for what seemed like a very long time. "Enjoy it while you can, buddy," whispered the Lieutenant. "That's your last leak."

Finally, Mr. Mustache buttoned up and walked slowly back toward his companions. He was in no hurry, and he took his last steps in an ambling lazy sort of shuffle.

The Lieutenant blocked out everything except the picture in his scope.

"Here he comes, sir. On my mark, sir," said Roberto, his voice as tense as the moment.

The Lieutenant exhaled slowly. In his sights the tall man remained motionless, intent on flicking some insect off the sleeve of his uniform. The crosshairs nicely quartered his chest, and the Lieutenant began to caress the trigger of his big Viper.

Roberto began the count. "Four, three, two, one, Mark!"

BOOM!

The heavy recoil of the Viper knocked the Lieutenant off the sight picture for an instant and when he looked back he saw a scene from Hell. The tall man was still leaning against the Humvee, pinned there by the gaping wound in his chest, but Mr. Mustache had not been so lucky. Roberto had been a millisecond early with his count, and the big bullet had passed through the poor man's skull just in back of his nose, blowing open his face like a bursting sack of rotten tomatoes. His mustache was gone and the place where his mouth had been now gapped open in a final scream that was carried to them faintly on the favorable breeze. He began to run in a flopping, senseless circle finally falling at the feet of the teenage Fidelista, who had gone from dream to nightmare in an instant of waking.

Quickly the Lieutenant shifted the crosshairs to the boy's head, but this time, in his anxiety to take the shot while it was there for him, he jerked the trigger.

BOOM!

An angry buzzing sound passed directly over the boy, and he looked wildly about for its source. By some sixth sense he looked directly at their firing point as if he could actually see the men who were killing him. Only at the last moment did he think to run for it, but he was too late by a heartbeat. The Lieutenant had regained the sight picture and his composure, and as he squeezed off the shot, the rock solid crosshairs foretold the boy's doom.

BOOM!

This time, the scope revealed the boy, tossed to one side, dead in an instant, no longer concerned about the strange buzzing he had heard or the other dead man lying at his feet.

"Oh my, God! Oh my, God!"

It was Roberto. He had witnessed the last three seconds in the crisp detail provided by his spotting scope, and now he was trying to fight down the nausea that overwhelmed him.

"Just like turkeys," marveled the Lieutenant, unable to keep the terrible thought to himself. "Did you see that, Corporal?"

"Yes, sir. 'Fraid I did, sir."

"Well, that's how turkeys act when you headshoot 'em."

"Those weren't turkeys, sir."

"No, of course not. No. But there is a similarity there," he said awkwardly, knowing how he must be sounding to his partner. His hands were beginning to shake, and he realized to his chagrin that he was experiencing a sense of elation rather than the guilt and revulsion that he had expected to feel. There was something about the act of killing in this godlike way that he found thrilling. Striking down an enemy with such unassailable force at such a great distance, was like wielding one of the thunder bolts of Zeus, and he knew for the first time why so many snipers continued to practice their craft as long as the Army would let them.

"Sir. We'd better get down there and clean up a little bit, sir. We don't want Father T.J. and the Bacas to see how this really went down."

They hurried down to the roadblock and dragged the three bodies into the brush. There they stripped off the undamaged uniform and laid it out neatly on the ground beside the Humvee. Roberto kicked some dirt over the blood, which had puddled beside the fire, and then he pulled out his pistol, pointed it toward the sky and fired three quick shots.

39

It took Boss Beckwith most of the day to see that his men and their families were properly protected from the attack he feared might be coming that night. He saw to it that the ammunition and fuel supplies were dispersed and that his people were bedded down in various old mine shafts up and down the steep-sided canyon. Finally he made the rounds, inspecting the shelters and giving the men a little pep talk at each one.

His last stop was deep within the old Hootenany Mine, where the Hackers Brigade, was based. This team of twenty-five or so oddly matched young men and women had been operational for only a few months, but they had already caused the Statists more trouble than the rest of the Patriots' forces put together. Like the short-wave radio network, the proceeds from the lucrative cigarette smuggling operations had been used to purchase high-powered computers and software for these young wizards to play with. Armed with these, their weapons of choice and their own, nearly preternatural skills, the Hackers spent their days invading the servers and mainframes of the bureaucrats, corrupting their databases and stealing their secrets. Usually they were able to commit their small acts of sabotage without even being detected, but when they wished, they could go on the offensive, spreading their own brand of mischief and mayhem throughout the entire central government.

Boss Beckwith was completely out of his element among the members of the Hacker's Brigade. His military posture was in sharp contrast to their casual individualism, and though he was well aware of how effectively they had bedeviled the Statists, it was an effort for him to think of these young people as comrades in arms.

Not wishing them to sense this, he had cut short his visit to the young cyber-warriors and was preparing to make his escape when their unit leader, Captain Johnson, came forward with a shy young man in tow.

"Colonel Beckwith, sir, I'd like you to meet Malarkay, one of our best hackers. He has something he thinks you ought to see."

Malarkay fidgeted nervously with a page of computer paper.

"You're way out of uniform, son," said Beckwith, unable to ignore the "Frodo Lives!" sweatshirt the boy was wearing against the constant chill of the mine.

"Sweatshirts are pretty much the uniform of the day down here, sir," interposed the unit leader. "Malarkay here is only fifteen. Home schooled, weren't you son?"

Malarkay was intently studying his out-sized feet.

"Isn't everyone these days?" said Beckwith with a laugh.

"Nearly all my people are, sir," beamed Johnson. "Only the best down here in the old Hootenany."

"How did you like being home schooled, Malarkay?" asked Beckwith.

"All right, I guess. Regular school is pretty much a waste of time, they say."

Education, or the lack of it, was a favorite subject of Beckwith's and he was about to unlimber some of his favorite pronouncements on the subject, but Malarkay had begun thrusting the printout at him insistently.

"I wish you'd read this, sir. It might be important."

"What is it, son?"

"It's some traffic I intercepted through the Beijing node."

"Beijing?"

"Yes, sir. From the Chinese embassy in D.C., sir. They've been back and forth about someone they call Lotus for weeks and yesterday I found this."

Beckwith accepted the paper and pulled out his glasses.

"LOTUS AGREES TO TERMS," it said. "CONFIRM SUPPORT BEFORE 0900 HOURS G.M.T. MONDAY."

"What do you make of this, son?" asked Beckwith.

"No telling, sir."

"Well, I tell you what, son. I'll show this to a few folks and maybe we can figure it out. In the meantime, you tell Captain Johnson here if you get any more messages about this Lotus business. He'll see that I get the message right away. Right, Captain?"

"Yes, sir. Right away."

Malarkay looked pleased, but Beckwith was already moving toward the door. He did not have time for chitchat with anyone, not even a room full of whiz kids who were, in many ways the best hope of the future he was trying to create.

He turned at the doorway. "Fine work you people are doing here," he said, and then he hurried out. At the mouth of the mine he pulled out his two-way radio and placed a call to the radio station.

"This is Beckwith," he said. "We're firing up early tonight. I've got a lot to say so get that antenna way up there."

40

As Alejandro's new pickup truck rattled through the outskirts of Santa Fe, he took his eyes off the road long enough to make sure that Joselito was still asleep. The boy lay sprawled across the seat, his regular breathing almost audible over the sounds of the heavy tires on the pavement. This was just what his young cousin needed, thought Alejandro. The last twenty-four hours had been Hell, and he needed to sleep it off. When he woke up he would feel better.

Alejandro was feeling better too. Leaving the Fidelistas had relieved him of a load of guilt that he had not known he was carrying. All those devilish little bombs. Some of the innocent victims of those bombs had been people he had known before Emiliano arrived on the scene with his seductive promises of land and power.

Now those promises seemed empty and foolish, and Emiliano's power over him was completely gone. He was quite sure of that, but he was not so sure what he might do after making this break with the Fidelistas. For now it was enough that he was returning Joselito to his mother. There was also the matter of the little chat he had managed to have with his old friend Flaco Ulibari just before he left the camp at Truchas.

Alejandro had known Flaco all his life. As a child, he had earned his nickname because of a tendency toward baby fat, and as he had grown to adulthood, the name had become even more ironic with each new hole he punched in his belt to accommodate his expanding waistline. They shared the same view of the world having grown up together in the little village of Peñasco, so it was no surprise that Flaco should feel exactly as he did about the way the leader of the Fidelistas had treated his cousin, Paquita.

"I have no more respect for Emiliano," said Alejandro. "A decent man would know better than to do such things to a young girl like that."

"I wish I had your nerve, to just walk away," said Flaco.

"Maybe you better think about leaving too, Flaco. You saw what happened this morning. Those mojados would have shot us down like dogs."

"I couldn't believe it," said Flaco.

"If they ever really took over, they would probably shoot us just to get us out of the way."

"Men like that cannot be trusted," agreed Flaco. "But what can we do?"

"There is something important you can do for Paquita, compadre."

"If I can do it, I will."

"Get on that motor bike of yours and go to the church at Las Trampas. Leave word for The Brotherhood. Tell them about what Emiliano did to Paquita and where they are headed."

"Dios mío! The Brotherhood?"

"And why not? Emiliano and Peligro deserve whatever they get."

The Brotherhood was a protective society, a relic of seventeenth century Spain, kept alive in the wilderness all those centuries. It was best understood as a cross between the Elks Club and the Mafia, ready to assist widows and orphans, ready to rebuild homes and churches, but ready especially to defend the honor of women and punish their seducers.

"The Brotherhood will not like to hear about this," said Flaco with a smile.

"The car is still giving Peligro trouble, so if you hurry maybe there is still time for them to do something about this outrage."

"They will kill Emiliano if they catch him," said Flaco solemnly.

"I don't care about that any more, amigo. From today I am no longer a Fidelista. As far as I am concerned Emiliano can go to Hell."

And so, Flaco had lumbered toward the north on his little motor bike, while Alejandro had put the boy in the pickup and headed south.

Now he was headed for Ft. Marcy Park to see the destruction for himself. It was worse than he had imagined. Several burned out cars and pickups smoldered in the parking lot, while the area near the stage, where so many of the people had been crowding close for a front row seat, looked like a bombed out battlefield. Nothing remained of Zozobra except a splintered telephone pole atop which sat two of the many ravens that inhabited Santa Fe. Other ravens waited their turn in the nearby trees while others managed to find a few widely scattered morsels of flesh a long way from where most of the rockets exploded. Ignoring the somber looking birds, a few women were placing descansos of flowers and white crosses to mark where their friends or family members had died. There were dozens of these little memorials already in evidence, and Alejandro shuddered to imagine how the scene must have looked and sounded to Joselito while such destruction was actually taking place.

The boy began to stir, and Alejandro quickly drove away from the park and headed toward La Ciénega. Better that the boy should awaken to familiar scenes of home rather than to these reminders of death and destruction.

41

The former President was excited. The prospect of being back in Washington D.C. before another day passed had him so keyed up that he couldn't sleep. About midnight he got up, dressed, and called Montgomery, the old groundskeeper who doubled as his caddy.

"Meet me at the practice green in ten minutes with my clubs and a bucket of balls," he ordered. Then he put on his old Air Force One windbreaker and went out to meet him.

It was a beautiful night. The early season cold front that had worked its way across the Rockies had not yet made it to the Ozarks, and the stars glittered brightly beyond the hills. He switched on the security lights, and saw that Montgomery was already waiting for him.

"I hear you gonna be leaving us, Mr. President," said the wiry little black man as he pulled a club out of the bag and offered it to the former President. "Nine iron, sir?"

"Yes, Montgomery. I'm going back for a big speech. Maybe you can watch it on TV."

"Yes, sir. Well, I hope I can, sir."

Montgomery dumped the golf balls on the grass near the former President and walked down the lawn toward the practice green.

The first ten shots were erratic, and Montgomery had to cover a lot of ground to gather them all up. Then the former President found his groove and began to place the balls closer to the flag. He was just beginning to enjoy himself when a voice from behind him broke his concentration.

"Long day for your ballboy."

It was Agent Mathison.

"Jesus H. Christ, son! Don't sneak up on a man like that."

"Sorry sir."

"How did you know I was out here anyway?"

"Remember your ID implant, sir? Lets me know any time you leave the building."

"So, no sneaking around on you, I guess."

"No sir. No sneaking around and no getting kidnapped either."

"Tell me, son. Does my wife have one of these implants in her ass, too?"

"Not unless she requested it, sir. And I don't believe she has."

"Well, I'm damn sure she hasn't. She never was too fond of you security types in the first place. Me neither, for that matter. Seems like you boys are always under foot. Don't give a man much privacy. Like right now, for instance."

"I'm just doing my job, sir. Like Montgomery."

"Montgomery? Listen here now. Don't you worry about Montgomery. Why, he's as loyal a Mino as ever walked the earth."

"Mino, sir?"

"Jesus, son, where have you been? That's the very latest name our Black brethren have decided on for themselves. Get it? Mino? Short for minority? They claim it's not so racist. Myself, I like it 'cause it's nice and short…like Nigger."

This brought a great whoop of laughter from the former President, who was so amused by his little joke that he had to suspend play while he finished laughing.

"I wouldn't know about that, sir," said Agent Mathison. "I just know it's pretty late for both of you to be up."

The former President found the young man's concern for his caddy to be rather quaint. After all, he thought, Minos were always so eager to please. He had counted on their votes for years, and they had never let him down, trooping to the polls and voting for him and his fellow Statists in overwhelming numbers. No matter that some of the Statist programs actually did more harm than good, or that the Minos' situation never seemed to get any better. They would line up at the polls and vote for him and his Statists every single time, like so many sheep to be sheered.

Montgomery trudged up the hill with the bucket of balls he had collected.

"You're really layin' them in there now, Mr. President," he said encouragingly.

Agent Mathison watched him plod slowly back to his post.

"Sir, don't you think…"

Suddenly the former President rounded on him in a rage. He was taller than the Secret Service agent by nearly a foot, and his grip on the nine iron seemed suddenly threatening.

"Don't I think it's Montgomery's bed time?" he hissed. "Don't I think I ought to let him go back to bed? No, I do not, Agent Mathison! You people keep me down here like some kind of prisoner and then you presume to tell me when I can practice my own goddam golf swing."

"But sir, I only meant…"

"You think I'm using Montgomery. Well, here's the scoop, Mr. Secret Fucking Service Agent! Most people want to be used! They goddam well beg to be used! They want somebody to tell them what to do because they're too pea-brained to figure it out for themselves. That's why they elect people like me and my wife to tell them what to think and how to act. Shit! If it weren't for us, most folks would be running around like chickens with their heads off. They need to believe that some smart son of a bitch has got it all figured out and will tell them what to do and how to do it. And if they have to pick up a few lousy golf balls or do any other goddam shit we tell them to do, then that's a small price to pay for not having to think for themselves."

As the fury passed the campaign smile reemerged.

"Don't look so shocked, son," he chuckled. "I'm not going to eat you."

Agent Mathison needed a second to catch his breath. He had heard about these rages, but he had never actually witnessed one. He decided to try a peace offering.

"Sir. I just remembered. I heard by the grapevine that an old friend of yours is going to be on that flight tomorrow."

"And who might that be?"

"All I know is it's a woman, sir."

"A woman, you say?"

"Yes sir."

"How old?"

"I couldn't say, sir. All I know is that there'll be a woman on your plane."

The former President chuckled. "Well, I guess that's all we really need to know, isn't it?"

42

*P*ATRIOT RADIO IS ON THE AIR...

Hello out there, my fellow Americans. This is Colonel Dalton Lamar Beckwith of the Patriots speaking to you from somewhere in the Rockies. Tonight, I want to talk to you about how you have been robbed of your education.

My friends, the Statists and their supporters have been systematically tearing down our educational system for the last fifty years, and it is they who are responsible for robbing you of the chance to learn. They may talk about hiring more teachers and building more classrooms, but what exactly are all those teachers teaching in all those classrooms?

Not much! The fact is that today's students are receiving less of an education than ever before. Instead of being taught important lessons in history and civics or geography and science, students learn only the bare outlines of such courses. Worse than that, the little that they do learn is distorted by the dictates of political correctness.

The schools are also failing to teach the basic skills. Instead of being required to learn grammar and math or memorize spelling and vocabulary, students are allowed to slip by without really learning anything and without being properly tested. They are simply passed to the next grade according to their age and warehoused for another year with others who are just as poorly educated as they are.

It is not just the teachers and school administrators who are at fault. Publishers cater to the dictates of political correctness and produce inadequate textbooks that do more to indoctrinate than they do to educate. The works of the best authors have been removed from the literature books. Math books concentrate on the easiest problems. While history and civics texts are full of so much revisionist propaganda that the true story of our great country and its wonderful Constitutions are almost entirely lost.

If you don't believe how poorly you have been educated, just try to answer the following ten questions. Two generations ago any hardworking high school student could have answered most of these questions with ease. Can you?

A fifty foot guy wire attaches to the ground thirty feet from the base of a vertical tower. Can you determine the height of the tower from this information? If you can, name the formula you would use to make the calculation.

Name the two largest tributaries of the Mississippi River.

In the sentence "All girls love candy," what part of speech is the first word?

What does a Presidential veto do? Can a veto be overridden? How and by whom?

If you write out the number "twenty-five hundred-thousandths," how many zeros will you use?

What does the Tenth Amendment to the Constitution guarantee?

What did Eli Whitney invent besides the cotton gin?

Name the Shakespearean character who tries to wash blood off her hands while she is sleep walking.

Name the historical figure who said, "Give me liberty or give me death."

Sixteen divided by one half equals what number?

Be honest now. How well did you do? Not so easy was it?

Now you can understand why our so-called educational system is the laughing stock of the entire world. Our students have fallen far behind those of other nations and all because our teachers, school administrators and textbook writers have followed the lead of the Statists. We are becoming a nation of nincompoops. Millions of unmotivated children are being taught by masses of incompetent teachers. Yet the Statists, who claim that they care deeply about the welfare of our children and the quality of their education, have stood by and done nothing. Could it be that this collapse of our educational system is what the Statists wanted all along?

Consider for a moment how easy it is to deceive a poorly educated voter. Ignorant voters are easily fooled. Complicated issues confuse them. They look for easy answers and end up giving their votes to the best looking candidate or to the smoothest talker. They elect demagogues and crooks. And in so doing, they put our democracy and our Constitution at risk.

My friends, we can not long endure as a democracy if our citizens are poorly educated. According to our Constitution, sovereignty rests with all of us. We are the ultimate authority, not the Statists and their minions. But if our impoverished educational system renders us incapable of voting wisely, then the Statists will be only too happy to take the power from our hands, and tyranny will be only a short step away.

43

"Let's stop here," said the Lieutenant. "We need to be close enough to back them up real quick if they need us."

"Only about fifty meters," said the Corporal, eyeing the distance back to the Humvee, where the Bacas and Father T.J. were awaiting the arrival of Emiliano's car. Father T.J. was sitting in the Humvee ready to turn on the headlights at the crucial moment while Tony and Lupe stood around the fire trying to look like Fidelista guerillas.

"At this range, you're gonna need to aim real low, sir," said Roberto.

"I figure about six inches. Don't you?"

""Maybe even more," said the Corporal, settling in behind a juniper without bothering to set up his spotting scope. They put on their black stocking caps and touched up their face paint. Then they unpacked the tortillas and goat cheese, poured themselves each a small cup of coffee from Lupe's thermos, and settled down to wait.

Overhead, the final act of a brilliant sunset was playing itself out across the entire western horizon. Before the light faded entirely, the Lieutenant sat back and took in the scene. The Taos highway led off to his right toward the Rio Grande Gorge only a few miles away, while directly ahead, U.S. 285 passed straight through the deserted village of Tres Piedras heading toward Colorado. Esmeralda was parked out of sight behind the Dairy Queen, so the intersection and the roadblock looked just as it had that afternoon when he first saw it.

McDowell was thinking that the three men he had killed would have enjoyed the beautiful sunset, but he said simply, "Nothing like this in Tennessee."

"It's the dry air," said Roberto, reading his thoughts. "You can see a long way out here."

"So, we ought to be able to see any headlights a long time before the car reaches the roadblock, wouldn't you say?"

They had agreed that they would signal their friends with Father T.J.'s big five-cell flashlight when a car was coming. The idea was to make them stop and then to lure the driver out into the headlights where the Lieutenant could get a good shot at him. "Remember," he had warned them, "don't get too close to the target, and for God's sake, don't stand behind him."

Roberto shivered and zipped up his jacket. "It's gonna get pretty chilly tonight, Lieutenant."

"At ease, Corporal. Special Forces types do not complain about a little thing like freezing their butts off."

"At least we got plenty of good food," said Roberto. "The widow Zamora's husband must have died a happy man."

The Lieutenant suddenly found himself thinking about Mr. Mustache. Certainly he had not died a happy man with his face shot away like that, but what about the tall guy leaning against the Humvee and picking a bug off his shirt? He had looked as if he didn't have a care in the world before the bullet reached him. Surely the big slug would instantly stun a man, like the butcher's mall stuns a steer. One instant you were looking at an ant on your sleeve, and the next instant you were dead. No fear, no pain, no suffering. If he did his job properly, no one suffered. Hemingway had called it "the gift of death." But of course he was talking about shooting Cape Buffalo at the time. Even so, the principle was the same.

"Wouldn't you say he died a happy man?" said Roberto, pressing for a reply.

"Right," said the Lieutenant "I suppose he did. Or at least a fat one."

He took one of the tortillas, broke off a chunk of the goat cheese and chewed them slowly. The neon glow faded completely from the sky, and the little campfire began to cast the shadows of Tony and Lupe on the old Humvee.

"Stay sharp, Corporal, " he said. "They're bound to be coming along pretty soon."

44

The old Mercedes carrying Peligro, Emiliano and the girl was approaching the outskirts of Taos. Paquita sat opposite Emiliano in one corner of the back seat, her legs drawn up beneath her, ready to kick out if he made a move toward her. She hugged a tattered blanket around her shoulders in a futile attempt to ward off Peligro's insolent gaze in the rear view mirror.

Emiliano seemed to have lost all interest in the girl, at least for the moment. He stared out the window, contemplating the various disasters which had befallen him in the last twenty-four hours. The rocket attack had been bad enough, but that was to be expected. War was war. You attacked them. They attacked you.

That much was simple. Less simple was the strange way that Alejandro and the other native New Mexicans had acted.

He had watched Alejandro drive away with the boy that afternoon. He was not sure if he would ever see him again, or indeed, if he really wanted to see him again. The fool seemed to have lost all sense of loyalty. It was all because of the girl, of course, but he would never understand why Alejandro would abandon his high-ranking position with the Fidelistas for the sake of a brother and sister he hardly knew. The concept of family loyalty was foreign to Emiliano, especially when it involved the tenuous ties which bound together the huge extended families of the Sangre de Cristos.

Emiliano himself had never really had a family. He remembered his mother, of course, and the hovel where she had managed to raise him without benefit of a husband. But that was no family. That was just a misery to be forgotten. The truth was that the Zapatistas were the only family that Emiliano had ever known. He could recall the face of every man he had fought with in those early days, but he could not recall the face of a single uncle or aunt. Even if he could have remembered any of his relatives, they would have meant nothing to him at this point in his life.

Yet these New Mexicans seemed to put family connections before all else. He had seen proof enough of that in the gun battle that had nearly erupted in front of his very own quarters that morning. Such disloyalty was very troubling to him, and he wondered if he could ever really trust any of the men who had stood with Alejandro, ready to die for their stupid family loyalties.

"Jefe, look! Ahead there. On the right."

The tone in Peligro's voice brought Emiliano out of his thoughts. He saw that they were approaching an abandoned shopping center. Several small bonfires dotted the parking lot and each was surrounded by a group of men. Some carried rifles and a few were armed only with baseball bats. Beyond the fires he could see their horses, saddled and ready to go.

"¿Qué pasa aquí?" said Emiliano, studying the crowd as they drove slowly past.

"Hunters maybe?" said Peligro.

"With baseball bats?"

Suddenly Paquita laughed delightedly.

"Not hunters," she corrected. "That's The Brotherhood."

"Now the little bird chirps," said Peligro.

"They are hunting for me," she said with certainty. "Alejandro told me he would send them to help, and here they are. If they catch you, they will punish you both."

Emiliano had heard stories about The Brotherhood. Dark and bloody stories, which he had always assumed were concocted to frighten adulterers and wife beaters into good behavior. Now seeing them in the flesh, with their rifles and their horses, he began to wish he had never thought of abducting anyone, especially this haughty young girl who was laughing and waving to the horsemen through the rear window of his car.

"I think they saw us," she said happily.

"Let them look all they want," said Emiliano. "We have the car and they have only horses. We will soon be across the bridge and on our way to Creed, and you will be sorry you ever laughed at me."

45

Cho Lin Wok possessed many social graces, but table manners were not among them. When he was hungry, he attacked his food like a man who had not eaten in a week. Though he recognized the defect he did not seem to be able to correct it, blaming it instead on a kind of racial memory of the great famines his ancestors had endured. Whatever the cause, he had just downed a double order of General Tso's Chicken in typical wolfish fashion while his Secret Service body guard snacked on a couple of egg rolls and a bowl of fried rice.

Wok had developed quite an appetite during his tryst with the President in the Oval Office. After that, he had spent another two hours in the White House Communications Office waiting for his messages from Bejing. Only then, with the ghost of famines past gnawing at his gut, had he put in a call for Agent Sommers to escort him to his favorite Chinese restaurant.

During her first term in office, the President had worked hard to transform the Secret Service into a sort of palace guard. Personal loyalty to the President herself was the first and only requirement for a posting to the new Secret Service. Eventually, the same transformation had taken place at other federal law enforcement agencies. The FBI, the ATF, the DEA, and the Federal Marshall's Office all had eventually been blended into a semi-autonomous agency, which reported only to the President and was the Statist version of the Stassi or the KGB.

Besides loyalty, the President also had a mania for security, and early in her term, she had ordered that all the streets leading to the White House be closed to traffic just as Pennsylvania Avenue had been barricaded when the Statists first came to power. No cars or trucks were allowed within a half a mile of the building, and the White House staff was provided with golf carts to help them move about the area. When one of them left the security perimeter for any reason, he was required to take a Secret Service agent with him for protection. This had the double effect of increasing security and also providing an easy check on just exactly what various members of the staff were doing at any hour of the day or night.

So it was, that no one in the crowded little restaurant saw anything strange about a high-ranking White House official like Cho Lin Wok dining in the company of a burly young security guard like Agent Sommers.

"Would you like anything else to eat Agent Sommers?" asked Wok, after enjoying a rich Oriental belch. "I'm having some more of this delicious tea myself."

Agent Sommers gave up his clumsy attempts at using chopsticks and pushed his food aside. He had more important things on his mind that night.

"I'd like to ask a favor, sir, if you don't mind."

"I'm afraid I'm not in the business of giving out favors, Agent Sommers."

The young man persisted. "When the balloon goes up…"

Wok made sure his face did not betray him.

"Please speak more softly so that you are not overheard."

"When the changeover takes place," Sommers whispered hoarsely. "You know."

"This is hardly the place to discuss any rumors you may have heard, Agent Sommers. Surely I don't have to remind you that loose talk is not conducive to good security."

Wok motioned for the waiter and waited patiently as the man refilled his cup with steaming hot liquid from a beautiful porcelain teapot.

"You know what I'm talking about, sir," Agent Sommers said when the waiter had finally left. "What I wanted to say was that after the announcement, there are going to be some resignations."

"Resignations?"

"Not everyone is as loyal to the President as I am, sir. I believe I just proved that loyalty today. The little business with our friend the senator, sir? Remember?"

"Yes. Yes. Of course."

"Well, all I'm saying is that I won't be resigning, and if something should open up, like say, a slot for a section chief, then you might put in a good word for me, sir."

"Yes. Well, I can promise you this much, Agent Sommers. It has always been the President's policy to reward those who are loyal to her, and I will personally make sure that she is informed about your many efforts on her behalf. Of course, you will have to submit your paper work through regular channels."

"Understood."

"I think you can count on an enthusiastic reception for your request, however."

Sommers smiled. "Yes, sir. Thank you sir."

Wok waited politely while the agent finished his meal; then he called the waiter over for a second time and handed him a list. In a few minutes he returned with their bill and a sack of carryout cartons. Wok tossed some money on the table and handed the sack to Sommers.

"One more little chore on behalf of the President," he said.

"What's that?"

"Tomorrow morning at 10:00 o'clock I want you to pick up the woman at the address on this piece of paper. She'll be expecting you. Drive her to Dulles Airport, and see that both she and this food are on board Air Force II before it takes off."

"A little in-flight party?" winked Agent Sommers.

Cho Lin Wok smiled his most inscrutable smile.

"Something like that," he said. "Let's just call it a little surprise party, shall we?"

46

The beam of the big, five-cell flashlight alerted the Bacas and Father T.J. to the car, which would soon be coming into view. Tony threw some more branches on the fire while Lupe fetched two coffee mugs and placed them beside the coffeepot.

"Be sure and hold that rifle like you meant it, mi vida," said Lupe. "Look real tough."

"I am tough," said Tony. "You know that."

"Always tough but never mean. That's why I like you so much, mi amor."

"Are you all right?"

"Sure. I just keep thinking of what they did to that poor girl."

"You just think about staying out of the line of fire, querida. That's the important thing now."

"I love you, Tony."

"And I you, mi vida," he said, picking up the assault rifle and striking his toughest pose.

Meanwhile, Father T.J. was testing the headlights of the Humvee to make sure they were ready when they were needed. The beams penetrated far into the darkness and out there in the distance he thought he saw the glowing eyes of a large animal. Perhaps a coyote, he thought, or perhaps Henry Red Wing's mysterious jaguar.

The headlights might be ready, thought the priest, but was he? He knew that he might soon become an accomplice to violent death. Murder was perhaps too strong a word for what was about to happen, but someone would surely die and the part he had played in the killing would be undeniable.

He had been praying over this for the last hour, but now as the critical moment approached, he found his mind wandering. Henry Red Wing's talk of shape changers and mysterious footprints kept invading his imagination as he thought what might happen the next time he switched on those headlights. Would he see Emiliano frozen in their beams or would he see something from another world, with glowing eyes and the sleek body of a big cat?

He scolded himself for such foolish ideas. First a party to violence, he thought, and now a believer in superstition. What kind of a priest had he become?

The old Mercedes was in view now and approaching fast. As it neared the roadblock Peligro began honking the horn, but Tony stood stolidly in the center of the road, rifle in hand, motioning him to stop. At the last moment the big car skidded to a halt in front of the barricade and Peligro stepped out, shouting at Tony.

"Move this goddam barricade! Don't you know who we are?"

"You have to show some ID," insisted Tony.

"Listen to me, estúpido! I am telling you that Emiliano himself is in the car. He is on important business. Now let us pass!"

"Identification first," repeated Tony calmly. "I have orders."

"Would you like some coffee, señor?"

It was Lupe. She had recognized Peligro instantly and now stepped forward with a cup of hot coffee for bait.

Peligro ignored her and drew out his old Colt automatic. He smiled at Tony.

"Listen, pendejo," he said. "This is all the fucking ID you are gonna see. Now move your goddam barricades before I start shooting!"

He took a menacing step forward. But one step too many, for it put Peligro exactly where Father T.J. wanted him, and he switched on the Humvee's headlights.

Peligro blinked at the sudden brilliance. He froze for a split second, just long enough for the Lieutenant to settle the crosshairs of the Viper on his chest and begin to squeeze the trigger. But before he could fire, Peligro's instincts came to his rescue. He made a lunge for the shadows just as the Lieutenant fired. The big bullet passed harmlessly through the tail of his jacket as he ran.

Peligro's instincts could not save him from his fate, however; for his dash took him in Lupe's direction, and she was waiting for him. She was not fast, but she was quick, and like the soccer goalie she once had been, she moved to cut him off as she would have moved to block a shot on goal.

She splashed the steaming coffee across his face and grappled him to her bosom. With her right arm she held the little man in a paralyzing embrace that locked his gun hand at his side, and with her left hand, she stabbed the sharpened ice pick straight into his right temple.

Peligro stiffened, his eyes asking a garbled question as Lupe began to stir the ice pick through the thick pudding of his brain. The hand, that had once so efficiently carved away Paquita's little white bra now fell limply to his side, and the brain, which a moment before had held a perfect memory of those virginal breasts, went forever blank, drowned by the hemorrhage that followed wherever the steel probed. But Lupe was still not satisfied. She probed further, as she would have searched a turkey for giblets. Finally she found what she was searching for, and the contents of Peligro's bowels and bladder gushed forth in a foul smelling flood. Then she stepped back, letting his body fall from her and crumple to the ground.

"Oh señor," she said in a voice that sounded strange even to her. "You have made a mess in your fine, silk underwear. Perhaps now you are not so proud of it."

She was aware that Tony was running toward her, but before she could gather her wits, she heard the deafening roar of a large automatic pistol firing at them from the direction of the Mercedes.

47

Emiliano had been feeling better with each mile they put between themselves and The Brotherhood. The roadblock seemed an unimportant interruption in their journey and he had watched contentedly from the safety of the back seat while Peligro tried to clear the barricades. When the Humvee's headlights came on, Emiliano's attention sharpened, but he was not prepared for Peligro's sudden scramble for safety or the roar of the Lieutenant's big rifle.

What happened next, as Lupe took her revenge, sent him into a mindless panic. He scooped up the sack of ammunition clips, flung open the door on his side of the car, and pulled the girl out with him, firing wildly toward the campfire to cover his retreat. He dragged his hostage toward the back of the Mercedes. Paquita put up a fight, screaming and struggling to free herself until Emiliano pistol whipped her into unconsciousness, threw her over his shoulder, emptied another clip toward the Humvee, and trudged off into the darkness with no plan except to survive at all costs.

Lupe was suddenly screaming piteously, and if Emiliano had paused to look back in his headlong flight, he would have seen that his wild fusillade had drawn blood. Tony Baca now lay flat on his back in the dirt, blood oozing from a large exit wound in his chest.

SUNDAY
SEPTEMBER TWELFTH

48

The same patch of brilliant sunshine that had awakened Father T.J. the day before, now awoke Alejandro from a night of evil dreams and terrifying visions. At first he was totally disoriented, lying slantwise across the top of Father T.J.'s bed with only a simple blanket to ward off the chill of the little bedroom. Then it all came flooding back. He remembered that he was no longer a Fidelista. His first reaction was a natural sense of loss. After all, he had given a great deal of effort to being a good Fidelista and a great deal of loyalty to Emiliano. It all seemed rather pointless. There was still the question of his family's lands, of course. That had not been resolved, but he could see now that the Fidelistas were far more interested in the application of raw power than they were in the administration of justice. The road to regaining the Vigil Grant for his family led through the ballot box and not through the car bomb.

Then there was the matter of Emiliano's charm. Alejandro had been flattered to have been given so much responsibility. He had followed Emiliano about like a little boy chirping "Jefe" this and "Jefe" that, ready to cater to the great man's every whim. Thank God Emiliano had reserved most of his more murderous assignments for Peligro, judging rightly that the little Nicaraguan was far better suited to such jobs than Alejandro. At least he could give the man credit for being a good judge of character, he thought. He felt guilt for the lives lost to the Fidelistas only in an oblique sort of way. He had most often been left to mind the store, so to speak, while his boss and his friends had been out murdering people.

But now all that was behind him, receding rapidly in his mental rear view mirror, as it were. Before him the road ran straight and clear. He was as free to wander as the dust motes drifting through the beam of sunlight above his head. But wandering was not what he had in mind. He wanted to remain rooted there in the Sangre de Cristos living the life he had always led except that now he would have to try and make amends for some of the wrongs done to his people by the Fidelistas. It was a heavy load he had chosen to carry, but at least he had gotten off to a good start.

He remembered how happy Joselito's family had been to see him tucked up safely beside Alejandro in the pickup truck, and how reluctant he had been to tell them that Paquita was still missing and probably on her way to Creed. Not even his brave promises about The Brotherhood rescuing her had seemed to help.

They had invited him to stay for dinner, and while he enjoyed a double helping of posole he listened to little Ricardo tell his story about the rocket attack and the other rescue attempt being carried out by Father T.J. and the Bacas.

"You see, Mama," the boy had concluded, "everyone is trying to help us."

Then there had been the question of where Alejandro should sleep. It was not proper for an unmarried man, even a nephew, to stay overnight in the home of a respectable woman with no husband to guard her reputation. Instead, they had decided to presume on Father T.J.'s hospitality, and sent Alejandro to sleep in his small bedroom behind the chapel.

The boys had showed him the way, carrying a couple of blankets and a pillow for him to use. The little room was cozy enough and the bed was very inviting and soon after the boys returned to their mother, he had fallen into a deep sleep punctuated by dreams of mysterious horsemen pounding down endless arroyos on the heels of Emiliano and the girl. But there was more to terrify him on his first night of freedom than merely dreams.

In the dead of night he distinctly felt someone tugging at his blankets. He raised up on one elbow and looked toward the foot of the bed. There he saw the specter of Peligro, his eyes rolled back so that only the whites showed. Blood pulsed from a wound above his right ear as his mouth worked to form words that were no longer there. Frustrated, the phantom turned away and paced slowly toward the chapel, where it found its way blocked by some immutable force. Angrily it spat a mouthful of blood across the threshold onto the floor in front of the altar and once again turned its fearsome gaze on Alejandro. The ghost took two steps toward him and then, as if called away by a power it could not ignore, it gave a farewell salute and dissolved into the shadows like a dollop of cream blending into a cup of coffee.

Not even the dawn could dispel the vision of that awful phantom, and Alejandro hurriedly barefooted it across the cold bricks to check the floor of the chapel. There was no blood to be found anywhere. The floor was as clean as when the ladies had last scrubbed it.

Feeling somewhat better, he sat down in the first pew and considered his situation. The ghost of Peligro had reminded him that he was now a marked man as far as the Fidelistas were concerned. No doubt there would soon be a price on his head after the way he had confronted Emiliano. What was he to do?

The chapel seemed a safe enough place for the moment. He wanted to pray for guidance, but all that he could remember was a passage from the Act of Contrition. This he repeated over and over while his subconscious mind worked on his problem.

The smell of the ancient chapel soon brought his sister Flavia to his mind. She had cared a great deal for these hand carved saints and these pain-wracked crucifixes that decorated the churches of the Sangre de Cristos. Some of those same saints looked down at him now. They were every bit as dark as he was, with long thin faces like his and eyes full of the sadness of mankind. The single crucifix that hung on the wall behind the altar left no doubt about the humanity of its bleeding Christ or the pain of the spikes that nailed him to that cross. This was a Christ who harked back to a darker age of Inquisitions and processions of hooded penitents. Yet this was a Christ who was so loved by Alejandro's sister that she had given her life to him.

Alejandro had never really understood why his older sister had decided to become a nun. She had been an ordinary tomboy who loved nothing better than riding her horse or climbing the apple trees in their orchard. Then she went off to the boarding school run by the Sisters of Loretto in Santa Fe and the next thing he knew she had cut her hair short and was talking seriously about her vocation.

She believed that Christ had called her to be his bride, and with her family's blessings she had gone to live at the convent, emerging several years later as Sister Feliz, long black robes, stiff white cowl and all. The Order had tried her out at a series of hospitals around the West before deciding that they needed her close to home and assigned her to Tesuque Pueblo as a grade school teacher.

She had continued living at Tesuque and working with the children despite the neutrality of the pueblo people. The children had pleaded for their beloved Sister Feliz to be allowed to stay, and so she had. Tesuque Pueblo had become her sanctuary, and Alejandro was beginning to wonder if it might not become a sanctuary for her little brother, the former Fidelista, as well. With that small hope to carry him forward, he headed for his aunt's house to find what sort of breakfast awaited him.

49

Tony Baca was still alive. At least he thought he was still alive. He couldn't be sure about anything at that moment because his senses seemed to be operating in sequence like a radio tuning from station to station. One moment he might hear voices talking nearby and later he might only feel some kind of heat warming one side of his body. At one point he smelled the unmistakable odor of exhaust fumes, and another time he saw a glimmer of firelight reflected in the windows of Father T.J.'s old van, which had mysteriously materialized right next to him. What it all might have meant was a mystery to him, but at least he was pretty sure that he was alive. In fact, he felt fine. If he could just catch his breath he would tell them all that he was not in any pain. He would tell them exactly how it felt to be shot because it was really very interesting. One minute he had been running toward Lupe. Then he felt something like a padded baseball bat hit him in the back, and the ground came up very fast and slammed into his face as he tumbled to a stop. Now his cheek felt bruised and gritty, and he wanted Lupe to come and wipe his face with a wet towel like she did sometimes when he was working in the garden. He wanted Lupe to come where he could see her and touch her, but she was not there and he was suddenly afraid that one of those padded baseball bats had also found her and killed her.

50

After Emiliano's escape, the Lieutenant and Roberto hurried back to the roadblock where Father T.J. was giving Tony the last rites. Lupe was kneeling beside her unconscious husband crooning mournfully and stroking his forehead.

The two soldiers immediately set to work doing what they could do to help. First they got rid of the stench of Peligro's corpse by dragging it into the brush. Then they found the first aid kit and applied a dressing to Tony's wound. Judging by the look of the blood, they guessed that the bullet had missed his lungs, and Roberto was beginning to think that his old friend might have a chance to survive if he could make it through the first few hours.

"Shock," said the Lieutenant, the single word reminding them both of what they had learned in their battlefield trauma course. Shock could kill too, and Tony might easily die from that before the night was out unless they could find a way to keep him warm.

"More fire," said Roberto, and the two of them began foraging frantically for dead branches and piling them near the fire. Then they brought Esmeralda out from behind the Dairy Queen and parked her next to Tony to form a windbreak. Finally, they covered him with all the coats and blankets they could find.

"This fire is lighting us up way too much to suit me," observed the Lieutenant. "Emiliano could come back here and pick us all off from out there in the dark."

"That's what you might do, sir, but remember that Emiliano is a coward. He ran like a jack rabbit."

"Maybe he wants to get his Mercedes back."

"Not as much as he wants to save his skin, Lieutenant."

"You're probably right, Corporal, but it looks like your friends have everything taken care of here, so I say we get away from this fire and find us a spot where we can watch their backs."

That had been several hours before, and now the two soldiers were crouched in the ditch beside the highway watching for any sign of movement silhouetted against the clear night sky. There was no breeze but the temperature had plummeted during the night, and they were cold to the bone.

"I wish La Puta was here," said Roberto. "She was good for snuggling up next to on a cold night like this."

"I'd settle for a pair of those chemical foot warmers that really worked," said the Lieutenant.

"You could snuggle up with her too, Lieutenant. I wouldn't mind."

"It must be nearly down to freezing," said the Lieutenant.

"She wouldn't mind either," insisted Roberto. "She is very generous with her snuggling these days."

The Lieutenant waited, hoping the Corporal would tire of talking about his unfaithful wife. But his partner could not seem to get her out of his head.

"She's the reason I joined up. Did you know that, sir?"

"I suppose a lot of men have taken the king's shilling on account of a woman," said the Lieutenant.

"Taken the king's shilling?"

"Enlisted."

"There you go, talking that high brow Tennessee talk again."

"Sorry about that."

"Now where was I? Oh yea. Anyway, I joined up because I was afraid of what I would do if she came back home, you know?"

"You wouldn't have done anything really violent, would you, partner?"

"I wasn't afraid of beating her up, sir. I was afraid of taking her back. I couldn't be sure what I would do if she suddenly showed up and batted those big eyes of hers at me and said she still loved me and she was real sorry. "

"I see."

"People wouldn't have much respect for a man who took his wife back after everything La Puta did. So I just pulled up stakes and got myself out of there before I even had a chance to be tempted."

"No second thoughts?"

"No sir. I think I was born for this military stuff, only I just never knew it."

"Same with me, only I always knew it."

"Lucky for you."

The Lieutenant glanced toward the campfire where Lupe and Father T.J. were taking turns watching over their patient.

"I guess Tony is pretty lucky too," he said. "Looks like he's still with us."

"Tony's as tough as they come, but I'll be glad when we get him to a doctor."

"How's this for a plan, Corporal? About dawn we'll take the Mercedes and go looking for that girl. Give it one more try for an hour or two. Then we'll come back and help take Tony back to town."

"OK by me, sir. Let's just hope the heater in that Mercedes is working so we can thaw ourselves out while we're at it."

51

The President's vibrating pillow alarm woke her at six o'clock sharp. Next to her in the big bed lay a handsome young soldier. He was a member of the ceremonial drill team that performed at White House functions. Even in sleep he was stunningly handsome, as he should have been since he had been chosen as much for his clean-cut good looks as for his skills at close-order drill. His unit, composed entirely of good looking young men such as himself could put on quite a show for the VIP's.

That was only their public duty, of course. In private, they were expected to service the President, providing her with all the hard young bodies she might need to slake the pangs of nymphomania which had possessed her since her inauguration.

This particular soldier was one of her favorites, Private Benjamin Fogarty or Big Ben as she preferred to call him for reasons that sometimes became quite obvious. He was Mr. Saturday Night as far as she was concerned, and if he kept on performing as he had only a few happy hours before, she would certainly see that his tour of duty was extended.

She stretched away the dregs of sleep, luxuriating in the feel of the satin sheets against her thighs. Mr. Saturday Night could sometimes be coaxed into performing on Sunday mornings as well, but for now she resisted the temptation and retrieved her pink silk robe from the floor, where she had let it fall shortly after he had come knocking at her door.

She padded quickly to the bathroom where she sat herself down on the toilet and picked up the secure telephone on the wall nearby. She punched in a number and waited.

The man who answered sounded fully awake, even though it was three hours before dawn in western Arkansas where he had been awaiting her call. "Hello?"

It was her old friend Major Harwood, formerly of the Arkansas National Guard. Six months before she had ordered him to reopen old Ft. Chaffee as a secret training center for a select group of several hundred men drawn from the ranks of the FBI, the ATF and the U.S. Marshals. These men had volunteered for special duty under her direct command. They had been sequestered at Ft. Chaffee for months while they trained, and now they awaited only her orders before setting out on their mission.

"Joe, this is the President."

"Yes, ma'am. I've been expecting your call."

"This is it, Joe. This is your official authorization. Deploy the men."

"Deploy the men. Yes, ma'am."

"And tell them I said, 'good hunting.'"

"Yes, ma'am. I will."

"Just so they're all in place by tomorrow night."

"Don't worry, ma'am. They've got your lists, and they know what's expected of them."

"We're depending on you all to keep a lid on things, Joe."

"We will, Madam President. Don't you worry."

"I tell you what, Joe. When this is over I want you and Mildred to come up here to the White House for a little private R and R. You two can sleep in the Lincoln Bedroom if you want. It's lovely now that I've had it redecorated."

"Yes, ma'am. We certainly will do that. Thank you, ma'am."

The President hung up and returned to the bedroom where she found Mr. Saturday Night still sleeping peacefully. His arms were flung wide, and he seemed as defenseless as a baby. He was irresistible. Without bothering to shed her robe, she climbed back onto bed and knelt astride him. A nibble or two at his ear lobe was all it took to bring Big Ben to attention, and the President was soon fully occupied with putting him through his paces.

Thirty minutes later she lay back exhausted while Private Fogarty hurriedly dressed and let himself out the door. Soon she drifted into a satisfied sleep, while convoys of black passenger vans, each marked with a bright pink stripe, left Ft. Chaffee and began fanning out across America like a dark and threatening cloud.

52

Boss Beckwith was enjoying the best breakfast he had eaten in several weeks. Perhaps it was the altitude or a slight case of nerves about the crisis that he now felt sure was coming, but it seemed to him that on this particular Sunday morning his biscuits were fluffier, his gravy tastier, his eggs fresher and his sausage even spicier than usual.

Of course, Patriot food was always good food. The men and women who joined their ranks tended to be from small towns rather than from big cities. Many of them had grown up on farms or ranches where they had learned how to cook, preserve, and grow their own food. Smoked sausage and spiced apples were no mystery to them, nor did they have to go to the grocery store to lay in a supply of dill pickles or fresh bread. Here at Creed they learned to raise their own chickens, hatch their own trout, and even grew their own mushrooms. There were enough potatoes, carrots, and beets stored in the mines and enough sides of beef and pork hanging in the icehouses to last them through the coming winter. The Patriots had made a good life for themselves there in Creed, and Boss Beckwith was sad to think that it might soon be coming to an end.

"Sir?"

Beckwith looked up to see someone standing over him holding a tray full of bagels. It was Malarkay.

"Want a bagel, sir? They're just out of the oven."

"Much obliged, son," he said, choosing the smallest one he could find. "It's Malarkay isn't it?"

Malarkay sat down opposite Beckwith and pulled out a sheet of yellow paper.

"Sir, I've been getting a lot of messages this morning. From my stringers."

Malarkay had developed a network of renegade hackers who had agreed to alert him to suspicious goings on in various parts of the country.

"What kind of messages, son?"

"Reports of troop movements, sir. Well, not troops really, but men. Lots of men in lots of black vans. They're heading out of Arkansas in every direction. And every van is marked with a big pink diagonal stripe.

"How many?"

"A hundred or more, sir. And there are helicopters too. Black with a pink stripe just like the vans."

"They're up to something. That's for sure." He slapped the boy on the shoulder, in a man-to-man sort of way. "This could be important, son. I think you're onto something here, so stay on it and keep me posted. I'll be at the radio station for the rest of the morning. You can call me there."

"Yes, sir."

Malarkay made a good faith effort at a proper salute and hurried back to his computers, while Boss Beckwith called for his car.

At the radio station he picked up one of the tape recorders and walked up to the big trout pond behind the building where he sat down on the earthen dam and looked out across the huge valley which had been cut and smoothed by the upper Rio Grande.

There was something he wanted very badly to say. He was not sure whether it was going to turn out to be a rallying cry or a sort of funeral oration, but he knew that it was important for him to get it on tape.

He watched a golden eagle drifting slowly toward the far side of the valley, and its flight led him to a vision of people from all races and backgrounds. He saw them worshiping God, each in their own way–Mormons and Jews and Amish and Roman Catholics and Protestants. He saw farmers and ranchers working the land. He saw factory workers and miners laboring at their jobs. He saw fishermen on their boats and oil workers on their drilling rigs. He saw a nation of free men, not a selfish gaggle of special interest groups, competing for special favors. He saw a nation of confident men, not a mewling crowd of weaklings claiming to be victims of everything under the sun. He saw a proud people, who wanted to live free, not a docile people who were willing to exchange the risks of freedom for the certainty of slavery.

Slavery was not merely a concept to Boss Beckwith for like a growing number of Patriots, he was Black. His own family had once been enslaved. That was long ago in Alabama, but he had heard the stories that had been passed down and he knew what happens when one group of men gains control over another. The crushing power of the slaver over the slave was not just a fantasy to Boss Beckwith. As a Black man, Boss Beckwith valued his freedom above all else, and as an American he valued it for his fellow countrymen too.

Finally, he took up the tape machine and began to record what he feared might be his last broadcast. The eagle was a long way off now, but he could no longer see it because, as he was quite surprised to discover, his eyes were full of tears.

53

Since first light the Lieutenant had been driving slowly down the deserted highway while Roberto scanned the distance ahead for Emiliano and Paquita. To either side, the plains stretched out to empty horizons. There were no villages, no farm houses, no service stations. Straight ahead, the highway lead toward the Rio Grande Gorge, which ran like a long black brush stroke across the land. This separated their foreground of scrub bush and piñons from a background dominated by a view of Wheeler Peak beneath which the tattered old artists' colony of Taos waited impatiently for the return of the tourists. Not far ahead was the bridge over the narrow, three thousand-foot deep gorge. They had already decided that this was to be the limit of their search.

If they could only locate Emiliano and the girl, they planned to take him out with a single shot before he even knew they were there. Too bad that Paquita would have to witness the carnage that resulted when that huge slug crashed home, but that was preferable to blundering into some sort of stand-off where Emiliano could use her as a hostage.

Time was running out. Father T.J. had reported that Tony seemed to have grown weaker during the night. They had decided to take him to Tesuque Pueblo where there was a doctor, rather than to try and make it all the way back to La Ciénega, but they had also decided that the two soldiers should make this last rescue attempt before they headed back. The Lieutenant and Roberto had hurried off on their mission, leaving Father T.J. foraging for more firewood while Lupe lay next to her husband to keep him warm. Tony would have to make it to a doctor before the day was out or he very probably would not live to see another.

The Lieutenant stopped the car as soon as they had their first view of the bridge. He backed the Mercedes up and parked it where it would be out of sight. Then he and Roberto crept forward on foot until they reached a spot where they had good cover and a view of the whole panorama spread out before them. There they initiated a systematic search for the fugitives.

It was Roberto who found them.

"I got 'em, sir," he said excitedly.

"Where?"

"Just this side of the bridge in the ditch on the right. They're down behind that big chamisa. See?"

The Lieutenant shifted the Viper slightly.

"OK. I got 'em too."

He could barely make the two out. They were crouched behind the bush, and it looked as if Paquita was struggling to free herself from Emiliano's grasp. He was holding her down with one hand and stifling her screams with the other.

"I make it eight hundred and sixty yards, sir," said the Corporal. "No wind."

"If she could just get loose I might have a shot," said the Lieutenant with his eye still glued to the scope sight. "Right now they're too close together to risk a shot. I might hit the girl."

"Not very damn likely, sir. You can make that shot with your eyes closed."

"Let's just wait a minute and see what happens. Does it look to you like he's trying to hide from something?"

Roberto consulted his spotting scope.

"There it is. That's what they're hiding from, sir. See those guys on the bridge?"

A line horses was walking slowly down the centerline of the highway. Each rider carried a rifle or a baseball bat and wore a bright purple armband. The lead rider displayed a banner of the same color.

"What's that all about?" asked the Lieutenant.

The Corporal let out a low whistle. "If that banner means what I think it means, then our boy has a darn good reason to hide out. That, sir, is The Brotherhood."

"The what?"

"It's sort of a secret society. They're almost legendary around here. They go way back to the good old days of the Spanish Inquisition, and they take a real dim view of men who molest their women and children. They say if you rape someone or something, then The Brotherhood will come knocking on your door and make you wish the Hell you hadn't. At least that's what they told all the guys at Santa Fe High."

"And you think they're after Emiliano?"

"Looks to me like they're about ready to knock on his door right now. News gets around fast up here, Lieutenant, and the way they're armed, I'd say they're sure as shootin' after somebody. Wouldn't you?"

When the horsemen reached the near side of the gorge, they stopped and gathered around the man who was carrying the purple banner. They seemed to be arguing about something and not one of them even glanced toward the place where Emiliano and girl were hiding only about fifty yards away.

"If they come this way, we need to be gone before they get here, sir."

"Come on, guys," coaxed the Lieutenant. "Surely one of you is going to notice those two hiding behind that bush."

"Maybe they need a little hint, sir."

The Lieutenant looked at his partner and saw that he was grinning broadly.

"OK, let's have it," he said. "What have you dreamed up now?"

"Well sir, see that big light pole about ten feet this side of Emiliano?"

"Yep."

"Well those things are mounted on concrete pads. An H.E. round right in the middle of one of those would cause quite a ruckus, sir. Get them looking over that way for sure."

"No chance of hitting the girl either! Good idea, Corporal. All right then. That's what we'll do."

The Lieutenant extracted three red-tipped, high explosive rounds from his bandoleer and slipped them into the magazine of the Viper. Meanwhile, the rider carrying the purple banner began riding slowly up the highway in their direction as the rest of The Brotherhood fell into line behind him.

"Better hurry, sir. They're heading this way."

The Lieutenant brought the big rifle to bear on the base of the light pole and took a deep breath, letting it out slowly as he began to squeeze the trigger.

BOOM!

When he regained the sight picture he saw that he had missed. None of the riders seemed to have noticed the little spray of dust that had been kicked up by the bullet, but they had certainly heard the sound of the shot when it reached them. They came to a stop and looked toward where they were hiding.

"Not up here, you idiots!" urged the Lieutenant. "Look over there behind that stupid bush."

"Low and left," reported the Corporal calmly. "Must be a little wind down there we can't see. Give it another try, sir. Up about a foot. Right about the same."

The dry, professional tone of his spotter helped the Lieutenant settle down. He blocked out everything except the crosshairs hovering over the base of the light tower and squeezed the trigger with the gentle caress of a born marksman.

BOOM!

It was a direct hit. The cement block under the light tower simply disintegrated in a shower of fragments and a cloud of dust. With its support shot away the light pole began to lean toward the road. For a moment it hung there secured by a single stubborn bolt, and then it pulled free and crashed to the asphalt, directly across the path of The Brotherhood. Their horses shied and the riders reined them in as they tried to see what had happened.

It was then that they saw Emiliano. Panic had brought him to his feet, and he was covered with cement dust from the blast that seemed to have gone off right next to his head. Still dazed, he froze like a startled chipmunk, but there was no hesitation on the part of either Paquita or The Brotherhood. She darted out of Emiliano's reach as the horsemen spurred their horses into a gallop and came for him. Emiliano fired two futile rounds and then bolted, trying to escape that thundering charge.

Two of the riders ran him down like a steer in the rodeo ring. One of them launched himself from his saddle and took the fleeing terrorist to the ground so hard that the pistol flew from his hand. Before he had quite regained his senses they had bound his hands and were walking him back to the road where their friends were already making a fuss over Paquita.

"Right in the ten ring," exulted Roberto.

"So, do we go down and claim the girl?"

"No way, sir. They'd never give her up to a couple of strangers. Anyway, she's as safe with them as she would be with her family. They'll make sure she gets home in one piece. You can bet on that."

"And Emiliano?"

"He's their problem now, sir. I'm sure they'll know what to do."

Two members of The Brotherhood had dismounted and given their horses to Paquita and the prisoner. Paquita's mount was a beautiful Appaloosa, which she sat proudly, beaming at her rescuers. Emiliano, on the other hand, had been put astride his horse facing to the rear. He slumped awkwardly in the saddle like a man who already knew what fate awaited him. He would be made an example for others, and it would be a long time before anyone was foolish enough to mistreat another young woman as he had mistreated Paquita.

The horsemen formed into two groups, one escorting the girl and the other guarding their captive. As they rode toward Taos, Roberto began packing up his spotting scope.

"Well, that's that, sir," he said. "Mission accomplished. Now let's get on back and see if there's anything we can do to help poor old Tony."

54

"Are you sure this thing is bullet proof?" asked the former President inspecting the windows of the Government Issue Toyota that was taking him to Ozark International Airport.

Agent Mathison was behind the wheel, negotiating the busy interstate, which was crowded with families coming home from church or out for a day at the lake. Norton sat next to him with the document box while Montgomery followed in a van with the luggage.

"Latest composites, sir," said Agent Mathison. "It'll withstand anything up to an RPG."

"Which those Patriot assholes have plenty of, no doubt."

"Don't worry sir. Security has been real tight ever since you've been…" He briefly searched for a polite way to put it. "…visiting down here, sir."

The old man looked at his watch.

"Jesus! It's after noon."

"Don't worry, sir," said Norton. "You can't take off till 3:00 anyway."

"And whose big idea was that? I'm the former Goddam President of the United States! I ought to be able to leave whenever I want."

He knew he was sounding petulant, but the thought of some woman, any woman, just waiting for him on that little jet was driving him crazy. He loved sex on airplanes any way, especially if there was a little turbulence.

"They're probably timing your arrival for the best media coverage, sir," said Norton, who by now knew exactly what to say to placate the old man.

"Right you are, Norton," responded the former President right on cue. "I'm just real anxious to get back into action. That's all."

Agent Mathison winked at Norton in the rear view mirror but said nothing.

Their little two-vehicle caravan had slowed to a crawl by the time they reached the twin towers of the National Choice Center. The former President had made his last public appearance at the dedication of the combined offices of the Kevorkian Institute and the Women's Reproductive Rights Clinic almost two years before. His wife had come down to make a speech and do a little fundraising among the wealthy retirees at Bella Vista.

The two of them had stood there on the platform, holding hands and beaming at each other like a couple of lovesick school kids. It was a performance they had given a thousand times before, and it meant nothing. When they were no longer in the spotlight they went their separate ways, without a word to each other. That had been the last time he had seen her in the flesh. And for that matter, the last time he had seen the Choice Center.

The green glass facades of the two buildings gleamed in the sunlight and the ever present column of black smoke from the huge crematorium that served them both was being dispersed by a light north wind. The skies had cleared during the night, and it looked like it would be a good day for a flight. Not much chance of turbulence, he decided, but at least he would soon be in the company of a real, flesh and blood female for the first time in a long time. That was all that really mattered.

55

Cho Lin Wok was on his way to have lunch with one of his operatives. He had just finished filing his Sunday dispatches to Beijing and not even the slight threat of rain in the air could dampen his good spirits. In a few more hours the waiting would be over and there would be plenty to do, but not today. Today was the calm before the storm. It was a good day to relax and enjoy one of the many fine restaurants that the city had to offer, thanks to the vast sums that were squandered by the corrupt powerbrokers who gathered in the nation's capitol like so many vultures around a fresh kill.

Since his favorite restaurant was close by the Chinese Embassy, Cho Lin had decided to walk. He carried his expensive umbrella jauntily, like a gold-handled cane. There was a spring in his step and a slight smile on his usually expressionless face. He was as happy as only a subtle man can be when his most subtle ploys are about to bear fruit.

He was so happy, in fact, that he slowed his pace, allowing himself the pleasure of watching the seductive oscillation of a shapely young secretary's hips as she strolled along in front of him. Thus occupied, he failed to notice the powder pink sports car that started its engine the moment he emerged from the embassy. He was equally unaware when it pulled into the right turn lane and waited for him to cross Constitution Avenue.

At the curb, Wok took his eyes off the girl long enough to see that the lights were with him, and then he stepped into the wide thoroughfare. The sports car immediately completed its right turn and began accelerating toward him. Wok was fifty feet from the safety of the sidewalk when he heard the sound of the automobile bearing down on him. He spun around just in time to see a pinkish blur heading directly at him only twenty feet away. He made a lunge to the left, but not even his years of martial arts training could save him. The car struck him smartly below the knees crushing his legs like a pair of fried noodles and sending him arching through the air, his umbrella flying in one direction, his body in another.

It seemed to him that he was airborne for a long time. At last, as he began to descend toward a final, skull-crushing collision with the pavement, he caught a second glimpse of the car that had just run him down. Had he had more than a millisecond of life remaining to him, Cho Lin Wok would have laughed out loud, for the delicious irony of it all was that he had just been struck and killed by a speeding Lotus.

56

When the Lieutenant and Roberto returned to the roadblock they found Lupe and Father T.J. preparing a bed for Tony in the back of the church van. The wounded man was visibly weaker now, and they paused only long enough to report on the success of their mission before loading him into the back of the van and heading south. Esmeralda now took the lead, playing the role of ambulance for the first time in her long and illustrious career.

Father T.J. had told them that there was a small clinic in Tesuque presided over by a German doctor who was well thought of by the people of the village. He was an older man who had lived at the pueblo for a quarter of a century, and except for the fact that his name was Schultz and that he still stood ramrod straight and towered over all of his patients, he was a Tesuque man through and through.

"Get the keys to that Humvee," said Father T.J. "And bring the spare gas, too. If we expect them to help us, we should be ready to offer them a little hospitality gift of our own."

The little procession reached the checkpoint at Pojoaque after an hour of hard driving. Father T.J. asked the men waiting to check them through to contact Henry Red Wing.

"Tell him that I would like to meet him at Tesuque as soon as he can get there," he said and gunned the old van on up the hill.

Henry Red Wing was waiting for them when they braked to a halt in a cloud of dust and sand.

"What's the problem?" he said, trotting out to meet them.

"It's Tony," replied the priest. "He's been shot."

"I knew you guys were up to no good," grumbled Red Wing. "How did this happen?"

"I'll explain later," said Father T.J. "Right now we need to get him to Dr. Schultz."

Henry Red Wing walked over to the church van and looked in.

"Hello, Mrs. Baca," he said. "Tony hurt pretty bad is he?"

"He's been shot," Lupe said helplessly. "He's worse now than he was this morning."

Henry Red Wing turned back to Father T.J. "All right then, Father," he said. "You wait here while I ask the governor's permission."

He made a call on the little radio, this time speaking in Tewa, his native language. It took him what seemed like a long time to reach the governor, who was a very busy man.

The governor of Tesuque Pueblo wielded almost total power over his people. Each of the pueblos chose a headman to run their affairs and deal with the outside world. The Spanish colonists had first awarded these headmen the title of governor and officially recognized their authority. When the Americans took over following the war with Mexico in the 1840's, they wisely retained the same system, dealing with the pueblos through their governors and councils and treating them as semi-autonomous states. .

As a mark of this relationship, President Abraham Lincoln himself had presented the twenty-four pueblo governors with gold-headed canes to symbolize their rank. These scepterlike trophies had been passed down from one governor to the next and carefully preserved so that the current governor of Tesuque was able to display his in a glass case on the wall behind his desk. He kept a magnifying glass near by so that the People could read the inscription in the words of the Great Emancipator himself.

Once Henry Red Wing got the governor on the phone, it did not take long for him to reach a decision. He turned to Father T.J., smiling.

"The Governor says he would make an exception for you, Father T.J., considering the emergency. You and the Bacas can go directly to the clinic, but your friends in the Mercedes here will have to confine themselves to the recreation center. Agreed?"

"Is that OK with you, Roberto?" asked the priest

"Sure, Father. Whatever. I just want to get Tony on the mend."

"All right then," said Father T.J. "Lead the way, Henry."

The Pueblo itself was located in a small valley below the main highway. The dirt road followed Tesuque Creek down into the village where the land spread out to provide room for a small cluster of adobe homes and shops. In the early summer the little stream might be nearly bank full with snow melt from the mountain, but by the fall, when the snows were just coming again, it was nothing but a sandy stream bed. Still, wherever there was water for even part of the year, huge cottonwood trees were able to find a foothold, along with a variety of bushes and great tangled masses of honeysuckle.

Passing from the high desert landscape into this green and leafy world was like entering another continent, so far removed from the world around it that it was easy to see how the Tesuque People had been able to maintain their identity throughout centuries of Spanish, Mexican, and American occupation.

The village itself was a seemingly random collection of buildings. There was a barely discernable center consisting of a few two-story buildings on one side and a circular kiva on the other. A long ladder protruding from the center of the kiva lead down to an underground chamber where only the men of Tesuque were allowed to go and where they shared their secret rituals with their shaman. Between these two structures was a dusty square where daylong ceremonials were held to mark the passage of the seasons.

On the outskirts of the little village were several buildings of an entirely different style. These had been built with government money from the FHA and the BIA. There were a few anglo-style FHA homes, known to all as "fachay" housing. "Fachay" houses were built according to federal codes that required certain standards of safety and durability, yet produced houses that seemed ugly and out of place in the ancient village.

Some equally ugly community buildings had also been built with money from the BIA. One of these was a multi-use gymnasium, known officially as the Tafoya Center. It had recently been dedicated to the memory of the young marathon runner who had won a bronze medal in the 2012 Olympics and then speedily succumbed to the lure of drugs and the big city. It was a large barn of a building, painted a dull, adobe brown to obscure the fact that it was constructed entirely of steel. It could have served equally well as either a warehouse or a small factory. To one side was a fenced off playground where two youngsters were making a racket on the rusty swings. In front, the unpaved parking area served as the last resting-place for the pueblo's yellow fire truck.

It was here that Henry Red Wing brought the Lieutenant and Roberto.

"Looks like this is where you fellows are going to be staying for a while," he said apologetically. "Hope you brought your tooth brush and a change of clothes."

"The Marriott it ain't," said Roberto, eyeing the big gymnasium with disdain.

"Well, at least we've got TV for you," said Red Wing encouragingly. He pointed to a pair of satellite dishes on the flat roof of the building.

"Can you get CCN?" asked the Lieutenant.

"And CSPN for sports plus a lot of other channels besides," said Red Wing proudly. "Solar panels on the roof give us plenty of power for the day and charge up batteries for the night time too."

"How about that, partner?" said Roberto to the Lieutenant. "At least now you can catch up on your precious news."

57

Tony was drifting painlessly somewhere above the main altar in the old Guadalupe church in Santa Fe. From his unusual vantagepoint he could look down at everyone who had come to his wedding. It was a very large crowd as Santa Fe weddings went. There on the front row was his elderly Tía Carlotta, long since dead, sitting next to his parents and wearing the corsage of violets he had picked for her. There was his mother decked out in the dress she had made and wearing her best silver jewelry. And there also was his dad, looking stiff and uncomfortable in the new suit the women had made him buy for the occasion.

The procession had already begun and Lupe's bridesmaids were moving slowly down the aisle. They were beautiful young girls all dressed in satin gowns that rustled softly as they walked. Following them came Lupe herself, escorted by one of her uncles, standing in for the father who had deserted his family so long ago.

Lupe had been the dream of Tony's young life. With the possible exception of a certain 1987 Cutlass, there was nothing he had ever wanted as badly as he wanted Lupe. That she should want him too and would actually consent to marry him there in that huge church in front of all of their friends and neighbors was a miracle of such mind-numbing proportions that it did not bear examining. He merely accepted it as he did a beautiful sunset or a timely shower of rain, giving thanks to God and marveling at his good fortune.

Lupe was wearing a beautiful white wedding dress, and as she walked down the aisle she seemed to be bringing her own light to that dimly lit sanctuary. All eyes were upon her, but she marched on boldly, smiling broadly and looking straight ahead toward Tony, who was waiting nervously beside the young priest who was to marry them.

This was a moment of victory for Lupe. She had battled long and hard to preserve the purity which that snow-white wedding gown proclaimed. She was, after all, a beautiful young girl growing up in a society where machismo ruled. Ever since middle school she had been forced to guard her reputation. When Tony began to show an interest in her she was even more determined to remain a virgin because she wanted their marriage, if there was ever to be one, to be strong and lasting.

Tony, of course, was not thinking that far ahead. His natural urges were as fierce as any young man's, and he did his best to overcome her resistance. He did not relent and she did not yield. Instead, she made maximum use of her ever-present dueñas and a bevy of her girlfriends to out-maneuver him. When that failed, she reasoned with him. If that did not work she used laughter and tears, or as a last resort she fended him off with a fierce strength that always surprised him. Most of all she used his great love for her. They both knew that he would never do anything to hurt her, and so the contest was over before it ever really began.

By the time he and Lupe were seniors in high school, that very private contest between his desire to consummate their love and her determination to remain a virgin had become legendary. As a result he became the butt of the jokes of all his compadres. He suffered their teasing gladly, because he knew that any one of them would have traded places with him in a minute. The love of a beautiful girl like Lupe, a girl with enough self-respect and integrity to resist the temptations of the flesh for all those years, was a prize worth any sacrifice. Lupe, on the other hand, was secretly glad that Tony never stopped trying to break down her defenses, and she made sure that he never doubted that the prize he had failed to achieve during their courtship would be all the greater once they were married.

The blackness surrounding his dream undulated around him and suddenly he was no longer floating in the air but standing beside her at the altar, a part of his own wedding. He lifted her bridal veil and stared down at her lovely young face. It was the face he had loved all his life, the laughing eyes, the pert little nose, the high brow ringed by soft black curls, and the perfect mouth with a slight smile always ready to blossom on those lips. He bent to kiss those lips and found them as soft and warm as he remembered, and then he knew that he had to live. He had to stay with Lupe for the rest of her life. He fought to hold on. He fought back through all the pain so that the visions receded and he found himself floating again toward blackness.

Finally one of his senses returned. This time it was his hearing.

Lupe was calling out excitedly to someone named Dr. Schultz.

"Oh look, Dr. Schultz," she said. "He's with us again. Oh gracias a Dios!"

And then he heard a strange voice with an odd accent. Was it German?

"Ja," the voice said. "Now ve see if he is a fighter."

Something about the stranger's accent amused him. Not yet able to see, he imagined a Nazi in an SS uniform working over him. Was Heaven full of Nazis? Had he died and gone to Germany?

"Look, Dr. Schultz," said Lupe. "He's smiling."

"Dot's a good sign, liebschen," said the voice. "Dot's a real good sign."

58

After he finished recording his broadcast, Boss Beckwith took out the little book of ciphers that he had brought with him and laboriously began composing a message for Patriot enclaves all over the West. These would be broadcast over the short-wave and sent out across the Internet as a seemingly meaningless series of numbers. Later, the same message would be reduced in size and sent out to those same enclaves via the homing pigeons that were kept in a roost atop the old courthouse in Creed.

This was to be his final message to his troops. The officers to whom they were being sent had instructions to decode them only if they believed that Boss Beckwith had been killed or captured. They were to assemble all the men and women under their command and read out this last message in their presence so that everyone could hear his words at the same time.

Getting these orders into the proper hands had suddenly become a high priority for Boss Beckwith, and he had spent wakeful hours the night before deciding just what he could say. It took him far less time than that to encrypt the short message that was the result of his efforts. When he was satisfied that he had said all he needed to say in the limited space available to him, he hurried back to the radio station and turned them over to the communications officer with orders to begin broadcasting them that night. He made ten reduced copies on the Xerox machine and headed back to Creed, where he would deliver them to the woman who looked after the pigeons with instructions to send them out at dawn the next day.

Then he headed for the old Hootenany Mine to visit Captain Johnson and his hackers. He was hoping that Malarkay might have developed some more information about those mysterious black vans that he had reported leaving Ft. Chaffee that morning.

59

At that same moment one of the vans in question was pulling up to the federal courthouse in St. Louis, Missouri. Six large and muscular men dressed in identical jumpsuits climbed out and stretched themselves.

Their unit leader opened his black attaché case and produced six manila envelopes. "Welcome to KMOX land," he said to his men. "Here are your lists."

He handed them each a thick manila envelope, keeping one for himself.

"We'll take a few minutes now to study the dossiers," he told them. "Each team should have recent photographs of its targets along with exact directions to their homes or work places. There is also a rap sheet telling exactly what your man has done to get his name on this list. The Administration is very thorough. They have done their homework, and I assure you that there is a good reason why each of these individuals is on your list. Your job is to get these people out of circulation as quickly as possible. When you get hold of one, bring him straight back here and get him into an isolation cell before you start after the next one."

"Wheels?" asked one of the men.

"Zebra Team, there are two vans just like this one parked in the garage under the courthouse. Go get them and bring them here."

"They want this all buttoned up by tomorrow night?"

"That's right. The sooner the better. If we miss someone, we'll just have to keep after him until we get him. They don't want any loose ends left hanging around."

"What about coffee, sir?"

"While Zebra team is getting the vans, X-Ray team can fill our thermoses at the canteen in the courthouse. Get plenty of donuts too."

"Sir, would you review the rules of engagement one more time?" asked another of the men.

"We are keeping a low profile, so hold the muscle work down unless it's absolutely necessary. We'll have the element of surprise going for us, so you ought to be able to have your man cuffed and into the van before he knows what hit him."

"And if he doesn't go quietly?" asked the largest jumpsuit.

"In that case, you are authorized to use whatever force is necessary."

"Deadly force?"

"That's affirmative. Even deadly force," confirmed the man with the attaché case. "Like they told us at Chaffee, no one is going to second-guess us on how this operation was carried out. All the Administration wants is to have these folks out of circulation. Above all they don't want them showing up on the job or having contact with anybody after tomorrow night. If you miss them at their homes, you are authorized to wait for them where they work. Use any excuse. Tell any lie. Just get them out of there and into isolation as quickly as possible. That's all they care about back in D.C. Period. End of story."

One of the younger jumpsuits responded with enthusiasm. "End of story," he said. "More like end of the propaganda these guys dish out. End of disloyalty. End of disunity. It's an honor to be part of a team that is cleaning up this trash for the nation and helping Madam President when she really needs it."

The unit leader smiled. It was clear that the six months they had spent training these men had not been wasted.

60

The President had spent the morning rewriting her speech. The words were no problem. She could write the words, or have them written. It was the way they were delivered that counted, and for that she felt she needed a bit more coaching. Of course, no one was better at this sort of thing than her husband was. He was a genius at disguising his real intentions and striking just the right pose to win over his audience.

In spite of herself she was feeling a bit nostalgic, recalling the early days of their courtship. He had been both brilliant and charming, a man born among the Red Necks yet marked for greatness. After their wedding she had gladly tagged along on his rise to power until his uncontrollable lust for women had turned their marriage into a dirty joke. By then, however, they had tasted political victory and discovered how well they could work together to win elections. Rather than give up the chance for more victories and more power, they had continued living together for the sake of their careers.

It was as if they had each made a bargain with the Devil, and as is usually the case with such bargains, they had tasted immediate success. Election victories came easily after that. The former lovers blended into a smoothly working team that inexorably climbed the ladder of power, until even the Presidency was theirs. At that point the nature of the game had changed, for her at least. The drive to win power was replaced by her absolute compulsion to cling to it. Once she had been elected President, she wanted nothing so much as to hang on to that office, to keep it in the family, so to speak, as if it was hers by some kind of divine right. She had worked hard to get where she was, sacrificed love and family, and suffered great humiliation, so why should she let a few words written on a piece of paper stand in her way?

A quiet knock sounded at the door to her suite. She knew that it would be someone coming to inform her about Cho Lin Wok's unfortunate accident. Poor Cho, she thought. Too clever by half, as the Brits say. What had made him think he could carry on back channel negotiations with Beijing without informing her? If anyone was going to deal with the Chinese it would be her and not some self-important toy boy.

The knock sounded again and this time she headed for the door determined to give a performance as convincing as one of her husband's.

The report was brief. Dead. Killed by a hit and run driver. Police looking for a small pink sports car. No other description.

"Thank you," she said simply. "Thank you for telling me." And the messenger of bad tidings went away, never doubting for a moment that the President was both surprised and suitably saddened by the news.

61

Meanwhile, the former President was arriving at Ozark International Airport a full hour before his plane was scheduled to leave. His Toyota and the luggage van were passed through the security gate and allowed to drive out onto the tarmac where the twin engine Gulf Stream was being serviced.

"I believe I'll just get on board right now," said the old man, as excited as a teenage boy on his first date. "No use having you fellows wait around. You should be getting back to finish closing up."

Agent Mathison helped Montgomery load the suitcases and trunks into the luggage compartment of the gleaming white jet, and then he handed the dispatch box to the former President.

"I could get in big trouble for leaving you alone out here, sir," he said.

"Don't you worry son. It'll just be our little secret. OK? No one is going to bother to assassinate an old fart like me."

"It's been a pleasure working with you, Mr. President," said Norton, putting a hand on his shoulder. He knew the old man well enough to know there was no use arguing with him, and, if the truth were known, he was just as glad to be done with what to him had been a dead end assignment.

"It's not the end of the world, Norton. I'm just flying back a couple of days ahead of you. I'm sure we'll be seeing each other around the West Wing."

"I'm sure we will, sir."

"Montgomery?"

"Yes, sir, Mr. President?"

"You promise not to tell anyone the truth about my golf game. You hear?"

"Oh, I promise all right, sir. They'll never hear it from me."

"I left my nine iron in my locker, Montgomery. You can have it if you want."

"Much obliged, sir."

"And, Norton? I left an autographed copy of my speech on the desk. It's for you. Something you can save for your grandchildren."

"I'm not married, Mr. President."

"Well, you know what I mean, goddam it man! It's a memento. History in the making and all that."

"Yes, sir. Thank you very much, sir."

"I'd better go on board with you just to check things out," said Agent Mathison.

"Is that really necessary?"

"Yes, sir. It'll just take a minute."

"Well, all right. Let's get it over with. Goodbye, Norton. See you in D.C."

"Goodbye, Mr. President. Have a good flight."

Agent Mathison boarded the Gulf Stream and made a brief but thorough inspection of the cabin while the old man waited impatiently at the door.

"Come on, son. Let's not take all day," he said testily. He was anxious for them to leave before his mysterious traveling companion put in an appearance.

"Regulations, sir."

"Fuck regulation! You goddam by-the-book types give me a pain. Just finish what you have to do and get the Hell out of here."

The young man checked the tiny rest room and the flight deck. He checked the overhead luggage racks and he looked under the seats. Then he left without a handshake or a word of goodbye.

The old man gave them a perfunctory wave at the cabin door as the Toyota and the van drove off. Then he went back to make his own search of the cabin. The only sign of the mysterious woman that he could find was a Kleenex blotted with lipstick lying on the floor beside one of the seats. He picked it up and smelled it. It held the slightest whiff of a very seductive scent. That was enough to satisfy him until the real thing arrived.

He was checking out the big Presidential seat, noting with anticipation that it could be adjusted to a fully reclining position, when a small truck drove up beside the plane. A man, wearing the uniform of a local caterer, hurried up the steps. He seemed surprised when he saw the old man working with the seat.

"Coffee service," he explained, indicating the large stainless steel tank he was carrying.

"Fine," said the former President. "Do your thing."

The coffee man headed for the little galley, but the Former President paid no attention. He wondered why they had even bothered to put coffee on board since it was well known that he never drank the stuff. No doubt, his mysterious traveling companion had requested it, he thought.

After a few minutes the coffee man emerged from the galley.

"That ought to take care of you, sir," he said.

"Yes, well thanks very much."

The old man took some papers out of his dispatch case and made a great show of studying them while the coffee man packed up his tools and drove off in his little truck. As soon as it was out of sight, a young woman appeared at the gate and began ambling slowly toward the plane. She was a brunette who looked to be in her early forties. Her outfit was decidedly girlish. She wore a short skirt and a thin blouse plus a jaunty black beret perched fetchingly atop her curls.

All in all she made a very pretty picture, but unfortunately, it was a picture with no name attached to it. Even as she reached the bottom of the steps and he prepared to welcome her aboard, he still had no idea exactly who she was. She might have been any one of a dozen women from out of his past, but even as he had a closer look, her identity continued to elude him. Finally, he decided he would have to fall back on the old reliable "Honey" and "Darlin'" until his memory clicked in. It had always been his experience that women didn't care what pet names you called them as long as you sounded sincere enough.

As she reached the top step he offered her his hand.

"Well now, honey," he said. "You just come on in and make yourself at home. It's mighty nice to see you again."

62

Alejandro had arrived at Tesuque three hours before Tony was brought in to see the doctor. Through the good offices of his sister, the much loved Sister Feliz, he had been allowed to enter the pueblo on a temporary basis. The council would decide whether to honor her request for resident status for him, now that he had cut his ties with the Fidelistas. In the meantime, like all visitors, his movements had been restricted to the area around the Tafoya Center, and so it was that he was already there, stretched out on the sofa in the TV lounge when Roberto and the Lieutenant came in.

Alejandro raised up and peered over the back of the couch at the new arrivals. He recognized Roberto immediately. The two of them had competed against each other in the state high school wrestling tournament more than once. That had been a happier time for both of them before anyone had ever heard of the Fidelistas and their bloody insurrection.

He got up immediately and went to meet the new arrivals.

"Hey, Chavez!" he called out "What happened to that kid who could wrestle at one hundred thirty-five pounds? You don't look like you could pull the weight any more, Bro."

Roberto saw a familiar face, which he could not quite match with a name.

"Peñasco High," prompted Alejandro. "We wrestled in the state tournament two years in a row."

"Both draws. Sure, I remember. Alejandro Vigil right?"

"The same, only a little less stupid."

The Lieutenant was puzzled. Alejandro Vigil was supposed to be a high ranking Fidelista, yet here was his Corporal greeting him like a long lost brother.

"I heard you ran off to join the Army," said Alejandro, with a glance at the Lieutenant.

"And I heard you got to be a big man with the Fidelistas."

"Yea, well that's what I meant about being a little less stupid, Bro. The fact is, I packed up and left that rotten bunch of mojados just yesterday. The next one I see will probably take a shot at me."

"So you're what we call a non-combatant."

"Strictly neutral. Like these Tesuque people."

The Lieutenant offered his hand.

"Glad to meet you," he said. "I'm Sandy McDowell, Roberto's partner."

"Pleased to meet you," said Alejandro. "So how come you guys are out of uniform? Did you desert like I did?"

"We're here on sort of a recon mission," said the Lieutenant.

"You mean you're spies."

"Not exactly," said Roberto. "I'll fill you in later, but first tell us what happened between you and the Fidelistas."

"Can you believe it? That son of a bitch, Emiliano, who I thought was my compadre, he just about raped my little cousin, Paquita."

"She was your cousin?" said Roberto. "I didn't realize."

"What do you mean you didn't realize?" said Alejandro. "Had you already heard about what he did at Fiesta?"

"Yea, we heard. That's what recon is all about. I don't see how you could have put up with that pig all this time."

"Me neither now that I'm finally quits with those guys."

Roberto smiled. "We been reconning the hell out of things, Bro, and we know a hell of a lot. Like for instance we know that your cousin is safe."

"Safe? Are you sure?"

"The Brotherhood has her."

"No shit?"

"I saw The Brotherhood rescue her about four hours ago. They're probably taking her back home right about now. And they've got Emiliano too."

Alejandro slapped his thigh and gave a little yip of happiness.

"I guess Flaco got through to them," he said.

"Flaco?"

"Before I left, I sent an old buddy of mine, Flaco Ullibari, to tell The Brotherhood what Emiliano had done to my cousin. I figured they would want to know."

"You figured right. About thirty of them on horseback armed to the teeth."

"I wish I could have seen that."

"Come on let's get some coffee and I'll tell you all about it."

The two headed for the canteen while the Lieutenant excused himself and headed for the TV lounge. The "Breaking News" logo was flashing seductively on the screen, as CCN interrupted it's regularly scheduled programming for a special announcement..

63

The young newsman stood at the edge of a large, empty expanse of concrete, squinting into the afternoon sun and waiting for his cue. In the distance a Delta Airlines jet could be seen taxiing toward the main terminal a mile or more from where the CCN cameras had been set up. A large black limousine was parked nearby and beside it several vans were lined up ready to form a suitably impressive motorcade for the final leg of the former President's trip to the White House. Drivers and security people stood next to their vehicles talking quietly to one another, but besides them, only a few network camera crews and a dozen or so reporters had been allowed access to the area where the little Gulf Stream was expected to land. There were no crowds of well-wishers waiting to welcome back the former President. No signs were waving. No bands were playing. It was, in fact, a fairly lonely scene, but true to his art, the young newsman tried to inject a little drama into the moment as he began to describe what little was happening.

"We are standing by here at Dulles International Airport," he said, "waiting for the arrival of the former President, who will soon be returning to the nation's capitol after an extended stay in his native state. Rumors are flying in official Washington that he intends to launch several important initiatives upon his return to public life. Sources close to the President have refused to comment on any such possible plans. However, they have put the major networks, including CCN, on standby to expect an important address from the White House sometime tomorrow night. Informed observers believe that at this time the former President will make some important remarks about his reasons for returning to the nation's capitol."

"Air Force II is scheduled to arrive around six o'clock this evening. As you can see a microphone has been set up, and we have been told to expect a brief statement from the man who has been called the most gifted orator of the twentieth century. If time permits he may even answer a few questions, but I'm sure he will be anxious to climb into that limousine and head for 1600 Pennsylvania Avenue and a reunion with his lovely wife. We will be rejoining you as soon as his plane lands so you won't miss a word spoken by this man, who is so beloved by the people of his country. Until then, this is Mark Dobson with CCN television news, sending you back to our studios in Atlanta."

64

It was not a newscast but rather his Office that was occupying Father T.J.'s attention that afternoon. Like every priest he was expected to read a predetermined selection of prayers, scriptures and homilies each day. This was referred to as "reading his Office," and was a discipline which normally occupied a good bit of his time. However, the last three days had been so chaotic that he had been unable even to open the little missal that he always carried with him, and he had fallen behind in his duties. Now, with Tony momentarily out of danger and Lupe finally able to sleep, he had taken the opportunity to bundle up and go outdoors to look for a quiet place to read.

He found it on a bench beneath a Russian olive in front of the little clinic. There he opened the little book to the page marked by a worn red ribbon. The past three days had taken more of a toll on him than he realized, and before long the sharply minted words began to move dreamily across the crisp onion skin pages. Father T.J. blinked them back to their proper places once or twice before finally giving up. He was too tired even to read.

Prayer often acted as a restorative for him, so he knelt there in the dirt, his hands stretched out across the weathered bench like a communicant at the altar reaching for the Host. There were so many souls to pray for, starting with Tony and Lupe and the three young men they had helped bury just twenty-four hours before. He prayed fervently and with so much concentration that before long he began to fall into a sort of trance.

Suddenly he was no longer chilly, but sweating in the heat of a summer day. He was standing beside his own little chapel. In the distance he could see the afternoon virga winds kicking up dust from the arroyos and sweeping it toward him. The winds increased, throwing up bits of trash to sting his face and whipping his robes against his legs. Father T.J. clung to the doorframe while the tempest buffeted his little church. Then it seemed to pass, but in the moment of calm that followed he saw a slowly swaying whirlwind sweeping across the village, sucking up everything that was familiar and comfortable about his life, and scattering it beyond hope of recovery.

Father T.J. was helpless before this vision. The winds continued to rise until the little steeple gave way and the church bell bounded noisily down the corrugated metal roof to land beside him with a dull clang.

He knew that he was receiving a prophecy from God. God had chosen him to witness to these things like the prophets of old, bringing a message of doom to people who refused to believe.

As the vision faded he realized that he had fallen to the ground beside the bench. He rolled over on his back and looked up through the gray green leaves of the little olive tree. Here in the real world, there was not a breath of wind, but only the icy blue arch of the sky bisected by a single white con trail spanning it from horizon to horizon like God's exclamation point.

65

Farther to the east in a rainier part of that same sky, the former President's little jet was beginning a slow descent toward Dulles Airport. He was content at last. As his pretty little travel mate busied herself in the galley fixing them both a snack of egg rolls, he lay back in his seat basking in the afterglow of the first real sex he had enjoyed in a very long time.

He was trying to remember every detail of that feverish hour. Whatever had gone on, it was a pretty good performance for a man his age. All he could really remember was her hungry thighs and those coal black curls capped by that little black beret bobbing about in his lap like some kind of excited puppy.

God but she was good! Her tongue had instantly identified her to him as the young volunteer he had seduced during his wife's first campaign. How could he have forgotten a girl who could do that little trick she had with the ice water? Her name was Mary Jo something or other, he thought, but he wanted to make sure because nothing made women any madder than calling them by the wrong name during sex. In the meantime "Honey" and "Darlin" seemed to be doing just fine. Later he would have someone look her up on a database of campaign volunteers. Then he would get her a job somewhere in the White House. His little ace with a hole, he thought, greatly amused by his own sophomoric humor.

The telephone rang. He plucked the little hand set from its bracket, letting it ring a few more times while he tried to think who in the world might be calling him just at this moment. Probably something about security, he decided sourly, and answered the call with an irritated, "Hello?"

It was his wife.

"Hello yourself, Mr. Tough Guy," she said. "I didn't think you were going to answer in time."

"Well now, to what do I owe this great honor, Madam President?"

He watched as the girl emerged from the galley with a plate full of the egg rolls she had found in the little refrigerator. She was wearing nothing except the little black beret he found so fetching. He could clearly see her beautiful naked breasts swaying gracefully as she came toward him down the aisle.

"How do you like that little floozy I sent you?" said his wife.

"You sent?"

"You ought to know by now that nothing happens around here, unless I say so."

"Well, if you really want to know, she's just fine, thank you. First rate in fact. Too bad you missed the party."

"Yes, well I never cared much for going away parties."

"Don't you mean a coming home party? Your old man is returning to make sure you don't botch the job."

"No, my old man is not! My old man is going away."

A cold chill ran down his spine.

"You're not sending me to another one of those gulags are you?"

The sound of his wife's laughter was audible even to the girl who was bending over him now brushing his face with one of her nipples.

"No, my dear," she replied. "I'm simply sending you off. You'll be gone in about two minutes as a matter of fact. I just called to tell you what a complete jerk you are while I still had the chance."

The girl was urging one of her nipples upon him, but he pushed her away. Terror was beginning to take over his mind.

"What do you mean, 'I'll be gone?'" he shouted.

"Just what I said. 'Gone,' as in blasted to bits, blown to smithereens."

"Oh my God!" he shrieked. "You can't do that to me!"

"Oh yes I can. In fact, I already have."

"But you need me. You need me to help you sell it. The people will never stand still for it unless I convince them it's OK."

"You're going to give me everything I need in just about two minutes, my dear," she said. "Now why don't you just go gobble down one of those yummy little dick-sized egg rolls I sent. You ought to have just about enough time."

By some awful coincidence, Mary Jo something or other was actually offering him an egg roll at that very moment. It was all too surreal. Panic seized him, and he leaped to his feet, shouting into the little telephone.

"Jesus Christ! Are you crazy? Wasn't Santa Fe enough? The whole place torn up. All those people killed. What more do you want?"

"I want sympathy, you idiot. I want people to feel so sorry for the little widow that they don't even notice that she's tearing up their fucking Constitution."

He looked at his Rolex. It was two minutes until five. Suddenly, he remembered the coffee man and the stainless steel canister. Under the counter top in the galley, he thought. That's where it was. Maybe he could get rid of it in time.

"You goddam dyke!" he shouted.

"Don't hang up," she ordered. "I want to hear it go off."

"You stupid bitch! You'll never pull this off without me!"

And with that he leapt to his feet, sending the girl and the egg rolls flying. He took one step toward the galley before his unzipped trousers dropped down around his ankles, tripping him up so that he sprawled in the aisle, clawing his way forward as the seconds ticked away. At the door he pulled himself up and began searching desperately for the bomb. He found it under the coffeemaker, and as his last seconds ticked away he shuffled toward a window grappling it to his chest with one hand and clinging to his pants with the other. Thus it was that the former President was pounding on one of the little Plexiglas windows, mindlessly screaming, "OUT! OUT! OUT!" when the pound of C-5 finally detonated and he learned that death sometimes begins as a brilliant white flash.

MONDAY

SEPTEMBER THIRTEENTH

66

Part of the wreckage of the little Gulf Stream had fallen to earth in the middle of the huge U.S. Government marijuana plantation near Asheboro, North Carolina. The tail assembly had landed in the middle of one of the carefully tended fields. Not far away a portion of the pilot's compartment with its empty seats dangling crazily could be seen at the end of the long scar it had gouged through a million dollars worth of U.S.D.A. Grade A marijuana. The center section of the little jet simply did not exist except as tiny bits of wreckage that were scattered across the landscape along a wide path that extended for several miles to the west.

Shortly after the turn of the century the Statists had pushed through legislation resulting in the confiscation of over fifteen thousand hectares of prime tobacco growing land in seven Southern states. They justified these seizures on the grounds that the owners had been profiting from the sale of a product that had once killed thousands of children each day. Few people, except the families, who owned the land, raised any objection.

A few months later, the same Statist regime legalized the sale of marijuana, converted the tobacco fields into experimental farms, and began producing huge crops of the fast growing drug. These marijuana plantations were a gold mine for the Statists, who speedily eliminated competition for their product by taxing private growers out of business and by cracking down hard on the smugglers who were bringing the popular drug in from Mexico and the Caribbean. After that it was a simple matter to seize a few of the shuttered cigarette factories and to convert them to the production of marijuana cigarettes. These were packaged in sturdy, Federal Blue six packs and sold at post offices throughout the country.

Federal Farm Number Ten contained twenty-five hectares of cultivated land and a number of storage barns. A twelve-foot, chain-link fence topped by electrified concertina wire, surrounded the entire plantation with a heavily guarded gate providing the only access to the property. It was there that the news crews began to gather as soon as word leaked out about the location of crash scene. Soon TV vans from Greensboro, Charlotte and Raleigh were lined up waiting to get in, but the gate remained closed until the CCN crew from Atlanta arrived.

Out in the marijuana fields N.T.S.B. investigators were busily talking photographs of the wreckage and collecting bits of debris, which might help them determine a cause for the crash. The head of the investigating team was occupied only with preparing for the press conference that he had scheduled for noon that day. The questions on these occasions were always the same, but since this particular crash involved the former President of the United States, he wanted to make sure he got it right so there would be no embarrassing slip-ups.

Yes, it was the former President's plane.

No, his body had not been recovered. Only the remains of the pilot and copilot and certain other body parts which had yet to be identified had been located.

Yes, they had recovered the flight recorder, but it would take a few days to analyze the information it contained.

No, they could not speculate about what might have caused the crash. Eyewitness accounts of a high altitude explosion were not to be taken seriously and were of little value compared to the painstaking efforts of trained investigators.

Finally at 10:30 a.m. the CCN van came lumbering down the road, pushed to the head of the line, and gave the signal to open the gates. The TV crews swarmed onto the plantation. There they found squads of military police already deployed along their route and restricting their movements to a single road leading to the viewing area. This had been stripped of marijuana plants and roped off to prevent anyone from getting too close to the wreckage. The only good thing about it was that it overlooked the crash scene well enough to satisfy the needs of the cameramen. Next to the roped off area was the little stage that had been hastily erected for the press conference.

Some of the news people quickly set about raising their dish antennas and sending live feeds back to their studios. Others simply waited for the press conference, passing the time by complaining to each other about the special treatment which always seemed to be accorded to the CCN crews.

The press conference began exactly on time, and in the welter of questions that followed, no one noticed the black van with the pink diagonal stripe that drove quietly up the road and parked out of sight behind the stage. A man in a jumpsuit got out, walked around to the front of the stage and passed a slip of paper to the N.T.S.B. official who was running the show. He read the note and looked out over the crowd of reporters. He was obviously disappointed.

"Gentlemen," he said. "And ladies," he added with a little bow toward a female reporter in a tight red sweater. "I'm afraid this press conference will have to be terminated. All information from this location has been embargoed. Any further questions will have to be directed to our superiors in D.C. Thank you very much for your patience. You have fifteen minutes to load up your equipment and vacate the plantation. The guards will escort you back to the main gate when you are ready to leave."

There was surprisingly little protest over this rather highhanded treatment. Official interference with their attempts to gather the news had lately become the rule rather than the exception for these people and their bosses seemed powerless to prevent it. Everyone simply packed up and drove away, not stopping until they reached a favorite watering hole for media people in Greensboro.

Everyone that is, except for the girl in the red sweater. She was not only pretty but sharp-eyed as well, and she made her driver pull over as soon as they were a mile beyond the main gate and out of sight of the military police.

"Wait a minute," she said. "I think I saw something hanging from a bush back there. I'm going to go check it out."

She climbed down from the van and walked back along the road a little way. Then she struck off into the undergrowth and disappeared. When she reappeared a few minutes later, she was proudly wearing the fruits of her search. It was a cute little black beret, slightly singed but otherwise quite undamaged.

67

The familiar "Breaking News" theme on CCN drew Lieutenant McDowell back to the television lounge as he foraged for a breakfast of cold tortillas and beans in the kitchen of the Tafoya Center that morning. He carried his plate and a cup of coffee back to the TV lounge and watched CCN's expanded coverage of the plane crash that had taken the life of the former President. Reporters interviewed Statist politicians and left-wing pundits, all of whom praised the accomplishments of the man who had so unexpectedly met his end, apparently the victim of a bomb planted, as nearly everyone assumed, by a right-wing paramilitary group. Videotape of the crash site and the press conference was shown, and purported eyewitnesses were interviewed by telephone. All reported the same brilliant flash in the sky at about five o'clock the evening before. All, that is, except for one intense young man who claimed to have seen a flying saucer hovering over the area for several hours.

Roberto stirred from his sleep on a nearby couch at the mention of flying saucers.

"We being invaded by Martians?" he asked cheerfully.

"Looks like the Philander-in-Chief has been killed in a plane crash."

"No shit! And I always thought that old goat would be shot by a jealous husband."

"I made a fresh pot of coffee, and there's a few more tortillas."

"Now that you mention it, I guess I could eat something. Too bad Lupe isn't here to fix us another one of those great breakfasts."

"Somebody mention my name?" said Lupe. She had just arrived, carrying a shopping bag full of the food she had retrieved from Esmeralda.

"I knew you two might be getting hungry about now, so I brought some things to cook."

"How's our patient?" asked Roberto, springing up and helping her carry the food.

"Doctor Schultz says he's probably out of danger, so I decided to come up here and celebrate with some chorizo. Women get hungry too, you know."

"What a guy that Tony is!" said Roberto. "He'll be back chopping wood before we know it."

"Don't count my chickens before they hatch," warned Lupe. "You are gonna jinx us." Right now she was happy just to have Tony whisper her name and give her hand a weak little squeeze.

She headed for the kitchen with Roberto trailing after her with the bag of groceries.

"I hope you got enough in here for four," he said.

"And who is the fourth?"

"Alejandro Vigil from Peñasco."

"That name sounds familiar," said Lupe

"I knew him in high school. We wrestled against each other some. Then he became a muy importante Fidelista, but now he says he has left them for good."

"Why should we believe that?"

"Because he is also Paquita's first cousin."

"Ayee! That's where I have heard of him!" said Lupe. "So he is her own flesh and blood! No wonder he is quits with the Fidelistas! "

"He is even the one who called out The Brotherhood."

"Better and better," said Lupe. "I want to meet this fellow."

An hour later the four of them were sitting around one end of a long table in the dining room. The dishes had been stacked off, and the Lieutenant was writing his father a letter that might never reach him while his companions gossiped contentedly. All through breakfast an undefinable feeling of dread had nagged at him, and now, not even composing a letter to his far-off family seemed to help take his mind off his worries.

Suddenly the big front doors of the Tafoya Center swung open, and Henry Red Wing walked in with three teenage girls carrying mops and brooms. He set the girls to work cleaning the TV lounge, and headed toward the dining room.

"Looks like you all are getting along OK," he said. "Where's Father T.J.?"

"He's with Tony," answered Lupe.

"He is doing better?"

Lupe nodded. "Thanks be to God," she said.

Roberto glanced toward the girls who were hard at work. "You didn't need to go to all this trouble for us," he said.

"Not for you, my friend," replied Red Wing. "The Pueblo Council will be coming here to watch the big speech this afternoon, and the governor asked me to get the place ready for them."

"What speech?" asked Lieutenant McDowell.

"Haven't you heard? CCN has just announced that the President will be making an important speech from the White House at 6:00 o'clock this evening."

"Dios mío!" exclaimed Lupe. "That woman is not human! She should be mourning her dead husband instead of going on TV. What's so important she's got to make a speech about it today?"

"I don't know," said Henry Red Wing. "CCN only said it was going to be something about national security. With that bunch, who can say?"

"National security?" said the Lieutenant. "That's what they said?"

Red Wing nodded.

The Lieutenant frowned. The cloud of dread that had been hanging over him suddenly became more definable. "Great!" he said sarcastically. "I wonder what kind of hoops they want to make us jump through now."

68

The President took the White House elevator down to the entrance of the huge new bomb shelter buried deep in the bedrock beneath the White House lawn. She had ordered the existing bunker expanded during her first term so that it now extended all the way out under what had once been Pennsylvania Avenue and included, among other things, a small television studio from which she planned to deliver her announcement that evening.

It was now more than twenty-four hours since she had shared her husband's last moments via telephone. Whatever brief pangs of grief she might have felt for the father of her only child and her husband of so many years had long ago been covered over by her anxiety about the business at hand.

By now she was wearing her game-face, the steely-eyed look that told everyone to stay out of her way and to speak only if spoken to. As she moved about the West Wing, members of her staff ducked back into their offices or down hallways to avoid making unnecessary eye contact and disturbing her legendary concentration. When there was no place to run, they stepped quietly aside, earnestly studying the toes of their shoes in hopes of forestalling one of her famous tirades.

The elevator doors opened to reveal the office area of the bunker, a long corridor, painted battleship gray, with passageways branching to either side. Her office was at the far end of the hall, and she headed there now to review her speech one more time before the television crew arrived to prepare the studio for her broadcast.

She practiced her lines in front of a mirror, trying for a look that subtly blended elements of the grieving widow, the Virgin Mary and the stern dominatrix. It was no easy task. The dominatrix kept crowding out the widow and the Virgin Mary. She tried her best to subdue that part of her nature and let the softer, more feminine side show through. Perhaps a slight adjustment of her hair might do the trick, she thought. Something a little softer, a little less severe. She ordered the hairdresser on duty to meet her in the bunker right away. This was no time to hold anything back. The fat was in the fire, as her late husband used to say, and if a new hair-do would do the trick, then a new hair-do she would have and have it quick.

69

Lieutenant McDowell was enough of a diplomat to know that he should leave the best seats for the elders of the Pueblo, so instead of claiming a seat on the couch, he staked out a spot on the floor a little to one side of the big television set.

It wasn't long before Henry Red Wing came and hunkered down beside him.

"Father T.J. tells me you're a mighty fine shot," he said casually.

"Does he?"

"He says you can hit something as far away as a mile."

"Depends on what that something is."

"Something like our old friend, Emiliano?"

"Yea, well, that didn't quite work out," said the Lieutenant.

"Lupe told me that The Brotherhood has him now. She said you had a hand in that. Did you?"

"I guess you could say that," said the Lieutenant modestly.

CCN was running a review of the events surrounding the former President's death and the controversy over whether or not a terrorist bomb had caused his plane to crash into that marijuana field, but the sound was turned down and nobody was paying much attention.

"Do you mind if I ask you a question?" asked the Lieutenant impulsively.

"Of course not."

"Well, what I don't understand is how you Tesuque folks could remain neutral while a guy like Emiliano was running around on the loose."

"Maybe we figured the whole U.S. Army could take care of him for us," said Red Wing pointedly.

"Seems like we should have, doesn't it? Frankly, I never understood why we didn't. It was like we were just going through the motions, like we didn't really care whether we chased him out or not. It was like a repeat of the Bosnia thing, except not so bloody cold. A lot of good men killed and not much results to show for it."

Henry Red Wing stood up.

"Come with me," he said. "I'll show you some good men."

On the back wall of the huge meeting room there was a small memorial to the war dead of Tesuque Pueblo. A row of young men's photographs hung on the wall above a display case filled with medals, newspaper clippings and personal items donated by some of their families.

"These men all died fighting for the United States," said Henry Red Wing. He pointed to one young man in the uniform of the United States Marines. "This is Ben Two Eagles. He won the Congressional Medal of Honor for saving six other Marines from a whole platoon of Japs on Iwo Jima. By rights this place should have been named the Two Eagles Recreation Center, but his son was too modest to allow it."

"His son?"

"Governor Two Eagles."

The Lieutenant studied the men in the photographs. They were just boys really, wearing the dress uniform of their particular branch of the service.

"What do you notice?" said Henry Red Wing.

"No sailors?"

"What else?"

"This all goes pretty far back. The last man died in Viet Nam. There's no one here even from the Balkans campaign or the Cuban annexation."

"And why do you suppose that is?"

"No more draft? "

"The men in these pictures weren't drafted. They all volunteered to fight for their country."

"So what changed after Viet Nam?"

"The country changed."

"Go on," said the Lieutenant, sensing that the conversation was finally getting around to the thing that Henry Red Wing had been wanting to talk about.

"Did you notice that big old cottonwood tree out front?" said Red Wing.

"Yes."

"That tree is probably two hundred and fifty years old."

"OK."

"Its trunk is at least six feet in diameter and its main branches are as big as young trees themselves. But cottonwoods can fool you. Sometimes they just look strong. They may have cracks you can't see or rotten places in their hearts. You think they are just fine, and then one day you are out for a walk and a little wind comes along and down comes one of those branches right on your head."

"So what are you saying?"

"I'm saying that tree is a little bit like the United States, Lieutenant McDowell. Like that cottonwood, the United States may seem strong enough at first glance, but it's really gone rotten inside. There are splits and cracks all through it. Splits and cracks that can lead to disaster and that your government hasn't done a thing about repairing because they're more interested in telling everybody how to behave and what to think than they are in healing the divisions within your society. The worst part is that the American people don't seem to care. They're so busy playing their video games and chasing each other around the bedroom that they sit back passively and let the government take them over."

"You got that right."

"So is it surprising that our young men have lost the desire to fight for such a country?"

"I guess not," admitted the Lieutenant.

"Here in the pueblos we have not lost our way. There are no cracks and no splits. We still have our customs and our traditions. We are still one people, and we will hold onto our way of life no matter what your government does or doesn't do."

At that point the front doors swung wide and a dozen elderly men from the pueblo filed into the Tafoya Center along with their families and friends. They might have been a group of old friends coming to the recreation center for a game of cards. They were dressed casually, and wore no marks or symbols of their office.

"They don't dress like much," said Henry Red Wing, "but here come some men who really care about what's best for their people."

70

Emiliano was feeling very sorry for himself indeed. He had been trussed up with several yards of prickly horsehair rope and laid out on the floor of an empty stall in a horse barn a few miles from where he had been taken prisoner. No one was paying any attention to him at all, except for one young man who came in now and then to check his ropes.

Emiliano had watched enviously as the men of The Brotherhood made a great fuss over the girl. They gave her a hot meal and cold apple cider to revive her spirits. Then when she was ready, they sent her off toward La Ciénega with an escort of men to accompany her on the long ride home. Emiliano had seen her riding off on the Appaloosa, looking for all the world like some sort of Andalusian princess, sitting her horse with the grace of a lady who was accustomed to triumphal processions.

After that, Emiliano had been tossed into the filthy horse stall where he lay for a long time without so much as a chance to go to the bathroom. Of course, Emiliano was enough of a realist to know that matters of personal hygiene were of little importance now. He had no doubt that these men planned to kill him. The only questions were how and when.

He had been passing the long hours imagining the various possible modes of his own death. They might hang him, of course, but he hoped they would not. He had witnessed several hangings, and he thought it a very undignified way to die. They might put a bullet in the back of his head right here in the barn. That would be the most efficient way to do it, but Emiliano judged that these men would want a little more of a show for all their efforts.

Since they were a quasi-religious organization they might take their cue from the Bible and crucify him. That was it, he thought. They might crucify him and leave his body hanging there as a lesson to others. This was Emiliano's second favorite choice for the death he might prefer to die. It would be a painful and dreadfully slow way to leave this world, of course, but at least people would remember a man who had died on a cross.

By far his personal choice for a way to die would have been by the firing squad. He had long harbored fantasies about standing heroically before the guns of a firing squad. He would stand there looking coolly down the barrels of those guns–erect, fearless, refusing the blindfold and holding a final cigar clenched defiantly in his teeth. Perhaps after a final puff he would spit out the cigar and call out the orders himself. "Ready! Aim! FIRE!" he would shout bravely, and people would talk for years to come about the man who had gone to his death with such courage.

However he died, he hoped that his executioners would allow him to give a short speech before the sentence was carried out. He had been working on that speech for years, and he imagined that his last words would be so stirring that they would light the fuse of another more successful revolution in a few decades. Perhaps those guerillas would be known as Emilianistas. Perhaps they would bear his image on their banners.

Such hopes sustained him throughout a long and thirsty afternoon and into the evening. When his rope checker finally came back to look in on him, he asked for a drink. The rope checker left briefly and returned with a small bottle of water, which he held to Emiliano's lips.

"Tell me," Emiliano croaked after he had managed to swallow enough of the water to moisten his throat. "What is going to happen to me?"

"You will see," said the rope checker curtly.

"Why is it you are taking so long? I have been tied up for more than a day."

"Doc Quintana is helping deliver a calf in El Rito. When he comes you will find out."

The rope checker turned to leave, but Emiliano called out to him in a hoarse sort of whisper.

"Wait," he said. "Don't go."

The rope checker stopped and looked back at him.

"What do you want?"

"I have a treasure," blurted Emiliano, his dreams of courage forgotten in a final desperate attempt to save himself. "It is a huge trunk full of Navajo jewelry and diamonds. Pearls too and other jewels. More than one man can carry. I could give you a map. I could take you there if you will just untie me."

"You will give us your jewels when Doc Quintana gets here," laughed the rope checker. "And we won't need a map to find them either."

He went out without another word and Emiliano was left to puzzle over what the rope checker had thought was so funny about his jewels.

If this Doc Quintana was delivering a calf, he must be a veterinarian, thought Emiliano. *But why were they waiting for him?* Was he the leader of The Brotherhood? Was he some kind of judge?

Then it came to him. Suddenly he knew why they were waiting and why the rope checker had laughed. The realization filled him with an awful terror that burst from him in a strangled cry. He strained against the horse hair rope and screamed. In spite of all his dreams of bravery, he screamed so loudly that the men of The Brotherhood could hear him as they warmed themselves in front of their campfires. They listened to his endless screams and smiled at each other with grim satisfaction.

71

As Lieutenant McDowell looked back on the event later that night, he had to admit that he was not really expecting the bomb shell that the President dropped near the end of her speech. No one could have predicted it, except perhaps the shaman who had been warning of bad times ahead.

The telecast started out predictably enough with a brief review of the former President's life: his childhood in a small Ozark town, his years as governor, and the highlights of his Presidency. There was no mention at all of the many scandals that had dogged his two terms in office or the scores of famous and not so famous women who had been linked romantically to him. It was just the sort of boilerplate obituary that all the networks kept on file to help fill airtime before the telecasts of the funerals of celebrities and political figures. This was followed by a full fifteen minutes of some equally boring remarks by CCN's news readers and correspondents, who droned on lugubriously about the former President's legacy, his place in history, and his legislative record. Finally they launched into a discussion of how stoically the President herself was taking the news of her husband's death and closed by speculating fatuously on what message she wanted to deliver to the American people that night.

Finally, as the appointed time approached, the pundits wound up their remarks and the picture on the big TV set changed to a close-up of the American flag waving in the breeze. The strains of "America the Beautiful" filled the air, and some one in the back of the room began loudly humming the "National Anthem." A few people applauded and then the picture changed to a live shot of the floodlit White House and everyone fell silent.

The feed from the bunker studio opened with a long shot of the President seated at a beautiful, cherry wood desk. Behind her stood the Attorney General, the Secretary of Defense and the members of the Joint Chiefs of Staff.

The President was wearing a simple black dress adorned with epaulets marked with vivid pink stripes, which echoed the service ribbons worn by the generals standing stiffly behind her. Slowly the camera pulled in for a close-up so the viewers could appreciate the look of utter sadness on her tear-streaked face. The image of the bereaved widow was perfectly realized until she began to speak, and then only the most cynical among the nationwide audience would have said that they could still detect the hard, authoritarian edge beneath the emotion in her voice.

The President began her speech by thanking the people for their telephone calls and messages of support. Then she went on to speak of her late husband and how his greatest concern had always been for the safety and security of his people. She emphasized how much the recent troubles in the West and the Southwest had concerned him and how he worried about the increasing amount of violence and disorder in the country as a whole. This was why he had decided to return to public life, she revealed, to help put a stop to this drift toward anarchy and insurrection.

There was more, of course. This particular President tended to talk on and on once she got started, and the Lieutenant had heard much of what she was saying before. He was beginning to pay more attention to the young men who were horsing around at the rear of the crowd then he was to the President's voice. Then he realized that she had begun to talk about what she referred to as her husband's assassination. This brought him back to full attention as she went on to claim that she now had proof that her husband's jet had been brought down by a bomb planted by those she referred to as right-wing extremists. She further stated that a splinter group of the Patriots had already claimed responsibility for the assassination and were threatening more.

"As you know," she went on, "both a member of my personal staff and a distinguished United States senator have recently been killed right here in our nation's capitol. We may soon have evidence that these killings were really assassinations as well. Who knows who may be attacked next? Who knows what the dangerous future holds for us, my dear friends? This is a serious moment in our nation's history. A moment, which requires determined action on my part and steadfast loyalty on yours. Even in the midst of my personal tragedy I know that I must act to protect you and those you love as dearly as I loved my poor dead husband."

Here she paused to regain control of her emotions and to wipe a further tear from her eye. "Now therefore," she continued, her voice rising with excitement in spite of herself, "I hereby declare a state of emergency and suspend the Constitution of the United States. This will enable me to take the sort of steps that may be necessary as I try to combat the terrible violence of these anarchists. I will govern under martial law only so long as it takes for your government to put an end to the extremist activity that now threatens us all.

The Attorney General to my left and the Secretary of Defense to my right have both advised me that this step is necessary if I am to have a free hand to deal with these terrorists and protect our country now that it has come under attack. Of course, I pray this will prove to be only a temporary interruption in the normal operations of our government, but I honestly believe that this is the best way, indeed the only way, to insure the safety of you and your children."

An audible gasp came from the small crowd gathered in front of the television set when the President declared martial law. For a moment everyone was frozen in disbelief, and then old Ben Two Eagles, the governor of the pueblo, stepped forward and briskly snapped off the television set. He turned to face the members of the council and the rest of the crowd that had been watching the speech.

Governor Two Eagles was tall for a Tesuque man, and in the small TV lounge, his anger was almost palpable. He took a minute to compose himself before he spoke.

"I will listen to this no longer," he said. "This witch wants to tear up the Constitution, and I say to her, 'No! No, you will not do that!' We Tesuque people cannot survive without the guarantees written into that great document. Long ago our ancestors threw off the rule of the Spanish because they tried to enslave our people. Then the Americans came with their Constitution and we learned how it could protect us from the lawyers and the politicians who tried to steal our land and our independence. President Lincoln sent us his words engraved on a walking stick to help us understand that we could be part of America under this Constitution. Thanks to that document we have been able to survive as a people for many years. We have preserved our customs and our language. Our children still grow up as men and women of Tesuque. Because of that piece of paper, America has protected us, and in return we have tried to be good Americans. Members of the council, I say that we must be good Americans now and protect the Constitution that protected us. We must resist this witch and her evil schemes. The time for neutrality is over!"

The eloquence of Governor Two Eagles stunned Lieutenant McDowell. He was not prepared for such a spontaneous oration or for the loud applause and the smattering of war whoops that followed it. Most importantly, he was not prepared for the sympathetic response the old man's words found in his own heart. The applause quickly grew into a rhythmic drumbeat of approval as the Governor's call for action began to take hold. He was so caught up in the excitement of the moment that it took him a few seconds to realize that Henry Red Wing was urgently tapping him on the shoulder.

"Be sure you don't leave here until we find out what the council is going to do," he whispered. "In the meantime, you had better figure out where you stand in all this."

72

Meanwhile the three powerful men who had been enjoying Stilton cheese and Madeira a few nights before were meeting in the same private dining room of the same exclusive club to monitor the President's speech. The Stilton cheese and the Madeira had been set aside and replaced by a magnum of the finest California champagne and a set of three tulip glasses. The reaction of these three men to the speech was far different than the reaction among the men of Tesuque. These three applauded politely as the President concluded with a tearful reading of "God Bless America," and the host for the evening reached for the ice bucket and popped the cork on the big bottle of champagne. He sloshed a celebratory portion into each of the three tulip glasses and handed two of them to his partners

"I believe this calls for a toast," he said.

They stood up and raised their glasses.

"Gentlemen!" said the host. "I give you the Queen!"

"The Queen!" they responded and drained their glasses to the last expensive drop.

"Give the old girl credit," said one of them. "That was a fine performance."

"Yes," said the host, "but she's still going to need a little help slipping this past the great unwashed. This sort of thing is liable to wake some of them up and her storm troopers aren't going to be able to put down all the protests."

"Don't worry. We've got everything covered for the next six weeks," said the third man, pouring himself another glass of champagne.

"Review the bidding, if you don't mind," said the host.

"Well," said the third man, "first there's the old man's funeral. Heads of state flying in from all over. Lots of ceremony. Lots of flag waving and marching bands. The public loves that sort of thing."

"And then?"

"Then, depending on conditions, we have a choice between the sudden and tragic death of a beloved movie star or two and the discovery of a threatening asteroid by our friends at NASA."

"I have a couple of movie stars under contract that I'll gladly donate to the cause," said the other man who was also starting his second glass of champagne.

"So do I," said the other. "Why don't we kill off two or three? They are such a fucking pain in the scrotum anyway."

"Now gentleman," smiled the host. "Let's not be selfish. Remember. This is for the Greater Good."

"I wish Babs was still around," said the drinker. "She loved the President so much she would have volunteered to fall on her sword for her if she thought it would help."

"Now there was a great funeral!" said the other. "That lady could really put on a show. Opposite the sixth game of the World Series and it still drew the biggest share for any funeral since that British royal got killed in that car wreck with her wog boy friend."

"OK, so a couple of celebrity funerals. No more than that or else it might look suspicious. And then right on the heels of that we get the announcement of the asteroid. We call it the Doomsday Rock or something. We ought to be able to stretch out the suspense for a couple of months on that, but what about after that?"

"How about our old standby, the economy? You know, we run a series of stories that make everyone feel like the Big Crash is coming. That always gets their attention."

"Remember the old man's first campaign? We put out all those stories about how the economy was going to Hell fast, and of course, we blamed it on his opponent."

"All people really care about is their pay check and making the payments on their fancy cars," continued the host. "No President has ever been reelected during a recession."

"But since we don't have to worry about elections any more..."

"We can get them as worried as we want, and they'll cling to our gal all the tighter. Like a nanny coming to rescue them from a bad dream."

"Sounds good to me."

"And if the protests continue we can always dream up something else."

"Like live sex on prime time TV?"

"That'll do it. We won't hear a peep from anyone if we give them a look at that." The host raised his glass a second time.

"The King is dead. Long live the Queen," he said amid a general chorus of laughter.

"What about live sex from the White House?" winked the drinker. "I hear the old girl is still fairly active in that regard."

73

Two heavily loaded helicopters were lazily circling over the rendezvous point at an altitude of ten thousand feet, fifty miles south of Creed. Soon a tanker from Kirtland Air Force Base would arrive and top off their tanks, enabling them to carry out their mission and return to their secluded little corner of the airbase well before dawn. They were armed with the same types of rockets that they had used at Santa Fe.

"Taco One to Taco Two."

"Go ahead."

"If your conscience is bothering you again, you can relax. I doubt these folks will be out partying like our friends in Santa Fe were. Over."

"Don't remind me. Over."

"This bunch probably has things pretty well buttoned up by now. Over."

"So why bother?"

"You know the answer to that."

"I know. Not a debate, right?"

"Affirmative. Not at all a debate."

And so the two unmarked helicopters continued to orbit each other until the tanker found them and did its job. Then they dropped down to tree top level and followed the moon lit ribbon of the Rio Grande north toward Creed and the Patriots.

74

Boss Beckwith's prerecorded broadcast followed the President's declaration of martial law by several hours. Now that the Patriots had been accused of being assassins, Beckwith knew that the time for propaganda was over and the time for action had begun. They would be coming for his people with both barrels blazing now, so it was with special interest that he listened to what he feared might be the last Patriot broadcast originating from this location.

At five minutes past the hour the music faded and his own voice came over the air with the familiar opening words of all his broadcasts, *"This is Colonel Dalton Lamar Beckwith of the Patriots speaking to you today from somewhere in the Rockies."*

Just then the intruder warning sounded. It was from the men at the forward observation post twenty miles below Creed. He picked up the radio and made contact.

"This is Beckwith. What have you got?"

"Helicopters, sir. Two of them. Tree top level. Headed your way."

Beckwith immediately sounded the general alarm sending everyone who was not already in the shelters running for cover. Then he picked up the telephone and called the radio station.

"This is Beckwith," he shouted. "I want you to break into the broadcast and patch this line through so I can get on the air live. Right now!"

He waited for a few anxious moments and then he heard the voice of his engineer over the radio.

"We interrupt this program for a special message from Colonel Beckwith, speaking to you live."

Beckwith turned off his own radio to kill the feedback and then he began speaking urgently into the telephone.

"We are under helicopter attack at our present location!" he said. "Repeat. We are under helicopter attack now! This is not a drill! All Patriot units should go to Condition Red Immediately! Prepare yourselves to be attacked wherever you are. Go to Condition Red, NOW!"

He repeated this message several times and then he went outside to see what was happening.

The helicopters had begun attacking one end of the barracks area and were methodically working their way toward the command post where he was standing. Several large fires were already burning, and many of the buildings seemed to have been completely destroyed, but the important thing to find out was whether or not any of his people had been killed.

He was just starting down the hill, to look for any dead or wounded, when a rocket came burning in and exploded twenty yards in front of him. The blast nearly knocked him down, but Beckwith managed to keep his feet and ran for cover behind a huge pile of firewood. Three more rockets came whistling in after that. These did not fall short of their mark and completely destroyed the command post he had just left, covering him with bits of debris.

He stayed where he was for several more minutes, but no more rockets came. The three that had taken out the command post seemed to have been the final three. Still, judging from the amount of destruction he had already seen, the helicopters had brought more than enough rockets to do the job. Most of the base that was above ground had been destroyed. Now he knew how the men at Pearl Harbor must have felt. One minute everything was normal and the next minute you were running for your life. Not a good way to start a war, he thought, but the men at Pearl Harbor had figured out how to turn things around, and he would just have to find the strength to do the same.

75

When Henry Red Wing returned to the Tafoya Center around midnight, he found the Lieutenant and Roberto in the kitchen talking to Alejandro. The Lieutenant was searching the static on his radio for distant stations.

"Something odd going on out there, Henry," said the Lieutenant. "About half of the talk show radio programs are running repeat shows tonight. Their hosts have called in sick or are just plain missing."

"And on a night when there's so much to talk about," added Roberto.

"We've got something to talk about," said Henry Red Wing, pouring himself a cup of coffee.

"What's that?" asked Roberto.

"You two are regular Army. Right?"

"Special Forces," said the Lieutenant proudly. "Same thing only better."

"Well, the Pueblo Council just voted to end their policy of neutrality."

Henry Red Wing blew softly across the rim of his coffee cup to cool the contents and allow the importance of what he had just said to sink in.

"That means that you two are going to have to leave pretty quick," he added. Then he looked toward Alejandro. "The same goes for you, amigo, since you were with the Fidelistas."

"I'm not with those cabrónes any more, man. After what I did to Emiliano, most of them would shoot me on sight. No lie. Anyway, your Mother Feliz is my sister Flavia, and I was hoping to live here with you all here at Tesuque. She was going to ask the council tomorrow."

"No second thoughts about the Fidelistas?"

"None."

"So I guess that just leaves you two for now," said Henry Red Wing, finally taking a sip of his coffee. "Now that we are no longer officially neutral, U.S. Army personnel are not welcome here."

"If you are no longer neutral, then what are you exactly?" asked Roberto.

"We are resisters."

"Resisters?" said the Lieutenant.

"Or defenders. It depends on how you look at it. We are resisting the Statists and defending the Constitution. You heard Ben Two Eagles. The only thing that kept us from being entirely swept away by you Yankees was that wonderful Constitution of yours. The idea of equal protection under the law–without that we wouldn't stand a chance. We'd be pushed off our land as soon as someone with connections decided he wanted it or wanted our casinos.

Then we would be scattered like quail. There would be no center for the Tesuque people. Kids would go wrong. Families would break up. Our language and our culture would die out and that would be the end of the our people. We would rather die now as Tesuque men than to see everything fall apart like that."

"But you don't stand a chance against a whole army."

"We believe your military will split. Some of its branches will split off like the branches on that big cottonwood tree I showed you. We will join with the ones who wish to fight for freedom. The other Pueblos will be with us too, and the Patriots, no doubt."

"I took an oath to defend the Constitution," said the Lieutenant to no one in particular, "not a dictator."

"Me too," said Roberto.

"You're right, about the Constitution, Henry," said the Lieutenant. "This isn't meant to be some temporary suspension. It's going to be permanent. They'll figure out a way to keep stringing it out until the people finally just forget about their Bill of Rights. They'll rationalize its loss like they rationalize everything else this government takes away from them."

"So much for freedom of speech," said Roberto.

"And the right to bear arms," said the Lieutenant. "What little is left of it."

"We can't very well go back to Kirtland," said the Corporal. "Someone back there would be just as happy if we never came back at all."

"So I guess that makes us resisters too," concluded the Lieutenant.

"At least we're pretty much unattached," said his partner hopefully.

Henry Red Wing smiled. "In that case," he said, "I expect the council will let you stay."

"Actually," said the Lieutenant, "I wasn't thinking of staying here."

"There is an empty "faychay" house all three of you could use if you wanted to," said Red Wing.

"Thanks for the offer, but I was thinking maybe me and Roberto would head north and try to hook up with the Patriots at Creed."

"We might be able to do some good up there," agreed Roberto.

"Sounds very tempting," said Henry Red Wing, "but don't go anywhere just yet. Sit tight for now because if you'll give me a chance, there may be a couple of things I can help you out with."

76

A full moon had risen over Truchas Peak, casting a pale light on the lower slopes. Here and there the moonlight glimmered on patches of snow left over from the first storm of the season. One of these patches was marked by the tracks of a big cat. They were huge pug marks, as big as saucers, like the ones Henry Red Wing had described to Father T.J.

The tracks had led to an overhanging bush where the ground was clear of snow and covered with a soft bed of pine needles. There slept the big cat that had made those tracks. A few hours before, a series of terrified screams had echoed up from the valley. The cries of wounded animals always whetted the big cat's appetite. They told her that she would soon find easy prey. For now she could sleep, but at dawn she would be up and out, searching the morning breeze for the inevitable scent of blood, which would lead her to the usual deadly rendezvous.

TUESDAY
SEPTEMBER FOURTEENTH

77

The President awoke to a beautiful morning. After a day or two of showers the buildings along the mall looked as bright and clean as a set of white China. She called for her morning papers and turned on the TV. A quick check of the headlines from several dailies and a few minutes watching the various network morning shows assured her that her friends in the media were still supporting her. Barely a peep of protest had been able to reach the public it seemed, and that had largely been drowned out by editorials supporting her take over. The largest Washington paper was running one on their front page congratulating her on her quick and decisive action to guarantee the public safety.

After breakfast she went to the situation room and checked on the progress of the suppression squads she had dispatched from Ft. Chaffee. The news on that score was good too. With only two or three of the units yet to be heard from, eighty-seven percent of the targets had either been silenced or eliminated. Many people were already in custody with more to join them soon. Three newspapers and six radio talk shows had been entirely shut down while two of her most outspoken critics on the news channels had been silenced permanently.

At noon she was scheduled to eat with her Chief of Protocol to review the arrangements for the various heads of state who would be coming to the funeral. It amused her that she should have to make such a fuss over these foreigners when she was the one who ruled the most powerful country on earth. Still, it was easier to flatter them than to fight with them, she supposed, and certainly she didn't need any foreign distractions just now.

She went back to her bedroom to dress for lunch, but before she sat down at her make-up table, she took a moment to find the notes she had been saving all these years in anticipation of her husband's funeral.

She pulled an old manila envelope out of the bottom drawer of her desk. It was stuffed full of clippings and photographs of other funerals. She had been secretly collecting these since the day when she had finally admitted to herself that her husband's womanizing was uncontrollable and that she would have to settle for a sham marriage with only a mutual love of power and money to hold it together. Since then she had been keeping this scrapbook as a sort of mental therapy.

Of course, the official plans for tomorrow's funeral had long ago been drawn up by the people who did that sort of thing. In the morning the closed casket, which was really quite empty except for a bit of the left leg and buttocks, which had been identified only because it contained the former President's ID chip, would be loaded aboard a hearse and driven slowly up the wide avenue toward the Capitol Building. There the bit of left leg and buttocks would lie in state until Sunday morning, when it would be driven to the National Cathedral. Along the way a sort of honor guard of children carrying baskets of flowers as well as scores of elderly, disabled, and homeless people, whom the former President was reputed to have been especially fond of protecting, would take turns walking, or wheeling, behind the hearse. Following a brief non-denominational service, the bit of left leg and buttocks would be flown back to the Ozarks for final burial in the garden of the Presidential Library.

Such were the official plans, but it amused her to read the notes she had been making for so many years in preparation for this day.

"No military crap," said one of them. "What the hell is a caisson anyway?"

"Get an old El Camino," said another. "Paint it black. He's had so damn much fun in the back of one of these, let's see how much fun he has when one is hauling him to the cemetery."

A sardonic smile touched her lips, but with that smile came the memory of the young man she had married, so brilliant and yet so out of control that no one could remain married to him and retain her self-respect. The thought brought a real tear to her eye, and for the first time in many months she wept for the life she might have had, something more fulfilling than the mad quest for power on which they had both embarked so many years before.

Then her own self-control, which had been perfected over the years by the need to keep up appearances, reasserted itself, and she locked the notes away. This was not the time for sentimentalism or weakness, she told herself. Maybe there would be a time later, when her position as President for Life was well established, but now there was no time for nostalgia. Now there was only time for resolute action.

As for love, she comforted herself with the knowledge that she could be sure of one thing at least. After the spectacle was over, after the heads of state had boarded their jets and headed home, after her staff had closed up shop and left her alone at last, there would always be Mr. Saturday Night.

78

Tony was sitting in an old wooden chair, soaking up the sun beside the front door of the clinic. Dr. Schmidt had decided that some fresh air would do him good, so he had directed Lupe to bundle her husband up warmly and help him out onto the front porch while they changed his bedding.

After she finished changing the sheets, Lupe went out to sit beside Tony, talking to him earnestly while she peeled potatoes for the soup she was making that night. She felt a tremendous need to talk to her husband now, as if the very act of talking was helping to keep him alive. The doctor may indeed have pronounced him out of danger, but she had come so terrifyingly close to losing him forever that she wasn't taking any chances. She talked on and on, chattering about anything and everything that came into her head, while Tony soaked up the sun and listened contentedly.

Suddenly the hollow clip clop of horse's hooves on the pavement interrupted her monologue. She looked up to see Henry Red Wing come riding around the corner of the clinic on a big cream colored stallion.

"Well, well," said Henry cheerfully, "looks like our patient is doing better."

"Yes, and tonight he is going to try to eat a little something solid," said Lupe.

The Lieutenant and Roberto rode up beside Henry Red Wing. They were mounted on frisky young ponies and leading a string of packhorses loaded with food, tents, ammunition, and weapons.

Hearing the clatter of hooves, Father T.J. came to the door to see what was going on.

"Where are you all going?" he said.

"I guess you heard that the pueblo is no longer neutral territory," said Henry Red Wing.

"Yes."

"Well, we are headed to Creed to join up with the Patriots," smiled Roberto. "We are deserters!"

"He thinks that sounds real romantic," said the Lieutenant, "as if we were pirates or something. Anyway, that's where we're headed. No telling what we're going to find when we get there. Patriot's Radio has been off the air since they were attacked last night."

"Why the horses?" asked Lupe. "Why don't you just take the Mercedes?"

"Because we'd make too good a target for the helicopters if they're still out hunting. Night or day doesn't make any difference to them. They'd be shooting at anything moving on that highway."

"So the Pueblo Council loaned them these horses," said Henry Red Wing. "And they sent me along to look after them, and to see how we can coordinate our efforts with this Beckwith fellow."

"Efforts?" asked Father T.J.

"You know," said the Lieutenant. "Resisting!"

"You heard about them declaring martial law?" said Roberto.

Lupe nodded.

"We have to do something," said the Lieutenant. "We can't just sit by and let them take us over." He took an envelope out of his shirt pocket and handed it to Lupe.

"My foot is much better now, thanks to you, Mrs. Baca."

"Lupe you mean," she said, wagging the envelope at him.

"I mean, Lupe," he corrected himself. "Anyway, would you please try to mail this to my dad if things ever calm down around here?"

"Your poor father," said Lupe. "Whatever will he think?"

"I know what he'll think all right," said the Lieutenant. "He'll think I'm doing the right thing. I'm sure of that."

Roberto dismounted and walked over to where Tony was taking everything in. He squatted down beside his old friend.

"Hey, Bro," he said, taking his friend's hand. "You get well real quick and maybe one of these nights I'll come sneaking back into your back yard to see you and Lupe."

"Don't go and get yourself killed," whispered Tony hoarsely.

"Did you ever know me to do anything stupid except to marry La Puta?"

"I know, but you watch yourself. Take it from me, compadre, getting shot is no damn fun."

"Don't you worry, Bro. I was always the one that didn't get caught, remember?" Roberto took his pony's reins from the Lieutenant and mounted up again.

"Just a minute."

It was Father T.J.

"A small blessing before you go," he said. "I would feel better. Please?"

"If you would, Father," said Roberto. "A blessing for all of us."

The little priest pronounced his blessing upon them, making an almost Papal sign of benediction in the air above their heads.

"Now," he said. "Go with God!"

And so they rode off, three men at arms, on horseback, ready to risk all for what they believed, a sight that had not been seen on those high plains for nearly four hundred years.

79

Later that same afternoon Emiliano looked out across the Sangre de Cristos toward Truchas peak. The Brotherhood had brought him to this barren spot high above timberline and left him there to die of exposure. His legs were trussed up with the same horsehair rope, and he was chained to a large rock with his arms splayed back around the icy boulder. The empty place between his legs where the veterinarian had made his cuts ached dully, and he wondered if the bleeding had finally stopped, not that it really mattered anymore. To the north another snowstorm was making up, and he knew that he would surely freeze to death during the night when the blizzard moved through.

A lonely way to die, he thought, with no one to appreciate any final speeches. Next spring the scavengers would find his body and his bones would be scattered so that no trace of him would ever be discovered. Nothing would remain except for those parts that the doctor had removed. Those tiny bits had been stored away carefully in a little jar, labeled with his name and the date. This had been added to a considerable collection of similar specimens, no doubt removed from other men who had suffered the same cruel fate.

Perhaps, he thought, those last remaining parts of his might someday become the focus of a legend, like the relics of a saint or the pieces of the True Cross. People would talk about his exploits and retell the stories of how his Fidelistas had ruled the Sangre de Cristos.

But even this comforting thought could not save him from the terrors of the death he was destined to die, for Emiliano was suddenly aware of a deep purring sound coming from somewhere to his left. He heard a guttural cough and turned to find himself staring directly into the golden eyes of a Mexican jaguar. She was huge, outweighing Emiliano by many pounds, yet she managed to get within five yards of him before he realized that she was there at all. She was watching him intently, her face hard and utterly without emotion, like a Mayan carving on an altar of stone. Emiliano knew he was staring his death straight in the eye.

She flattened herself even closer to the ground. Only the tip of her tail twitched spasmodically to signal the coming attack. Emiliano tried to remain absolutely motionless but his body betrayed him. He quivered uncontrollably as his breath began coming in frenzied gasps.

A final flick of the tail, a blur of gold and black, and she was upon him. The great leader was able to utter no more than a single terrified bleat as she pounced, closing her suffocating jaws over this throat. He thrashed against his chains and the unrelenting jaws. He tried to rip his throat away from those crushing teeth. Anything to gain another breath, another chance to fill his lungs. Anything…

The last thing that Emiliano saw was a single, golden eye, staring balefully down at him, and as his life ebbed away, he found himself wondering what had ever possessed this renegade cat to stray so far from her home south of the border.

80

The homing pigeon fluttered wearily onto the little roost, which had been built for it atop the firehouse in Springdale, Utah. The majority of the population of this unassuming little town at the entrance of Zion National Park had been watching for the arrival of that particular pigeon for several hours. If any state was truly Patriot territory it was Utah, and a goodly number of these men and their families had gathered in front of the town hall to await news of the fate of Boss Beckwith and the others at Creed. They knew a pigeon should be on the way with a message for them.

A cheer went up when they saw the little bird come swooping in over the pine trees. One of the men went to retrieve the message that was clipped to the pigeon's leg. He put on his eyeglasses and read it quickly to make sure it was legible. Then he mounted the steps of the town hall and looked out over the crowd.

"My friends," he called out, "this is what we have been waiting for. If you'll just settle down, you can hear Boss Beckwith's message."

The people quieted down immediately and moved closer to the steps. Even the children stopped to listen. The man with the eyeglasses held the little slip of paper so that it was in full sunlight. Then he read it aloud in a clear, strong voice.

"Patriots all! Our time has come! The issue of whether our children and our children's children will live as free men in a free society is now before us. It matters not what happens to us as individuals. It matters only that we save this Republic and the Constitution that has kept it alive for over two hundred years. We must defend the freedom that is our birthright as Americans so that we can pass it on to others. We must fight so that this wonderful nation, the last hope of a world full of the enslaved, will not fail. Even at the cost of our own lives we must oppose the tyranny that has suddenly descended upon us. Even at the cost of home and family, we must fight. We must fight to throw off the dead hand of the dictator and to protect the free society that our forefathers left in our keeping. This grave responsibility is ours and ours alone.

Difficult times are ahead of us, my friends, dangerous times, but I believe we are up to the challenge. I have faith in you, my Patriots. I have faith that you will not allow the light to fail, that you will fight on until you are victorious and our country is restored to it's former glory. As you embark on this crusade, I leave you with three words that have served other patriots well when freedom was threatened. Three words to live by and, if necessary, to die by. My fellow Americans, those words are DUTY, HONOR, and COUNTRY."

-finis-

APPENDIX A

Glossary of Spanish Words

Abrazo: a hug

Acequia: (ah/sáy/key/ah) A small ditch which carries water to irrigate a garden or an orchard. The "acequia madre" is the larger, "mother ditch" which diverts water from a stream or river and distributes it to the smaller acequias. Keeping the acequia system clear and free of trash and weeds is still an important part of life in parts of northern New Mexico, and men are appointed to oversee this task and organize the volunteer workers.

Cabrón: Literally, a big goat. An insult like Bastard or S.O.B.

Cojones: (co/hóne/es) Testicles or "Balls." A person said to have big cojones is being praised for his boldness and bravery. Note! While <u>cojones</u> are "balls," <u>cajones</u> are boxes. Mixing up these two words can create some very funny sentences.

Chorizo: (chor/eé/so) Spicy, Mexican sausage. Delicious! Try some the next time you go to the super market.

Curandera: (coor/ahn/dera) A woman who is skilled at the art of healing through the use of herbs and plants. A man with the same skills would be called a "curandero."

Dueña: (dwey/nya) A female chaperone. In colonial times, a well-bred Spanish girl would never go out in public unless she was accompanied by her dueña.

Flaco: Skinny.

Gordita: Literally, a fat, little girl.

Gente: (hen/tay) People, in a collective sense, as in the "people rule" or "all the people are here."

Huevos Rancheros: (way/vos) Literally, ranch style eggs. A two-fisted breakfast of fried eggs, Spanish rice, and refried beans, covered in chili sauce. Served with flour tortillas.

Jefe: (héf/ay) Chief, boss

Kiva: (kee/va) A circular ceremonial chamber, usually built below ground level and entered by a single ladder through a hole in the center of the roof. All of the New Mexico pueblos have kivas, as do many of the ruins which dot the state.

Madre de Dios: Mother of God

Mano a Mano: Literally, hand to hand, as in "hand to hand combat." In the world of bull fighting, a "mano a mano" match is one in which two matadors fight a series of bulls, first one man and then the other, competing to see which is the better torrero.

APPENDIX A (Con't)

Mojado: (mo/ha/tho) Literally, wet. An insulting term referring to illegal aliens or "wet backs."

Muy: (moó/ee) Very.

Padrecito: (pah/drey/ceéto) Literally, little father. An affectionate way to refer to a priest.

Peligro: (pel/eé/grow) Danger.

Pendejo: pen/dáy/ho) Fool, idiot. This is a fairly common insult, which, according to my sources, actually means "pubic hair." The strength of this epithet depends on circumstances and your tone of voice. As a general rule, this is the wrong thing to say to anyone who is bigger, faster, or better armed than you are.

Pojoaque: Rhymes with Milwaukee. A small pueblo north of Tesuque.

Posole: (poe/sole/lay) A traditional New Mexican dish made by slowly cooking pork roast together with chili, hominy, and garlic. Like black-eyed peas in the South, this dish is traditionally served at New Years.

Puta: (poo/tah) Whore.

Qué pasa aquí?: (kay pah/sah ah/kéy) What's going on here?

Quien es?:   (key/en/ ess) Who is it? The last words of Billy the Kid, who was shot in a darkened bedroom by a man he could not see.

Rayito: (rye/eé/toe) Literally, little lightening bolt or sun beam. In this case, a very ironic name. The Spanish word for lightening is "relampago." This is a wonderful sounding word, but I thought it was a bit too much of a mouthful for the name of a pet horse.

Triunfadór: (tree/oon/fah/thór) Conqueror, "triumphant one." Like "flaco" and "rayito," this is another slightly ironic name.

Mi vida: (me vee/the) Literally, "my life." A term of endearment, like darling.

Viga: (veé/gah) Large exposed beams that support a flat roof in pueblo style architecture. In most cases they are simply pine logs with the bark removed.

Virga wind: This is not a Spanish word but it requires some explanation for those who have not lived in desert climates. Virga is rain that falls from a thunderstorm but evaporates before it hits the ground. This evaporation of such a large amount of rainwater massively cools the air, which then falls toward the earth, creating a sudden wind seemingly from out of nowhere. Virga winds are a phenomenon of late afternoon since most desert thunderstorms don't build up until then. A small rain cloud trailing showers of virga ten miles away can produce thirty mile-an-hour wind gusts across a wide area.

Virgencita: (veer/hen/seéta) Literally, little virgin i.e. The Virgin Mary.

APPENDIX B

Due to circumstances beyond our control Boss Beckwith's regular broadcasts over Patriot Radio have been temporarily suspended. However, transcripts of his famous Memorial Day eulogy to our fallen war heroes are still available along with a copy of more examples of his high school proficiency tests for today's adults.

To obtain either a transcript of the Memorial Day eulogy plus a copy of one of his challenging tests, send $3.00 plus a SASE to Patriot Radio, 8535 Baymeadows Road, Jacksonville, FL. 32256.